THE FINAL REVENGE

A DI SCOTT BAKER CRIME THRILLER

JAY NADAL

INKUBATOR
BOOKS

Published by Inkubator Books
www.inkubatorbooks.com

ISBN (eBook): 978-1-83756-235-0
ISBN (Paperback): 978-1-83756-236-7
ISBN (Hardcover): 978-1-83756-237-4

Previously published by the author as Drowning.

PROLOGUE

He shivered as he stood rooted to the spot. The cold surroundings matched the feeling inside him. Empty, bleak, lifeless. Nothing had changed in all those years of careful planning. He'd tried to move on. Put it behind him. Had learnt to live with the tragedy. But the memories swirled inside his mind. They plagued him during waking hours, and they haunted him in his dreams.

Most of the time he felt nothing. The deep emptiness matched the frigid chill that gripped his heart. Why had it happened? Why had that one event, that one moment of lapsed concentration, robbed him of a lifetime of happiness?

He judged himself every day. Accepted the blame. But over the years, his thoughts had turned to the others. The ones who could have helped... but who hadn't. Why did they get to enjoy life?

It isn't fair.

He stepped back to admire his handiwork.

The tank was huge. Larger than expected. It had sat idle in this unit for over a year. As much as he'd wanted to reduce the breadcrumb trail, the manufacturers had insisted on delivery and installation. He'd given them a bullshit story about setting up a fish farm for tropical fish.

Everything was in place as he set up the camera feed. The disused barn was remote enough and hadn't been disturbed in over a year, so he was confident in the choice of location.

After opening his laptop, he logged on to the internet and searched for the camera feed to make sure it worked. When the screen lit up and showed the tank, his expression remained fixed as he nodded approvingly. The feed was laggy, and the recording froze every so often as he panned the camera around the barn. It wasn't ideal, but it would do. A price he would have to pay to hide his identity.

He sat on an upturned beer crate, waiting for the laptop to shut down. He pulled the photograph from inside his jacket and ran a finger over the image. He felt odd staring at a snapshot of his life – his *former* life. A time of happiness with laughter and plenty of smiles. Back then, his heart was bursting with love, happiness, and joy. Everything had been normal. Now, he didn't know what normal meant.

His throat tightened as if an invisible claw had wrapped its talons around it. His face reddened. Eyes grew heavy and his vision blurred. He waited but nothing came. There was no crying. No sadness. No tears.

He averted his gaze and stared off into the darkened space. He was nothing more than a cold, empty shell of a man, hell-bent on revenge.

The wheels had been set in motion many years ago. The seeds of destruction sown. But now, he wanted the man to suffer. He wanted everyone to suffer. For that reason, he'd been taking his time. So much of what he had done in recent years had been fuelled by twisted rage. His erratic thinking was now replaced by a cold, calculating mind.

Staring at the photograph once again, his most treasured possession, he exhaled. It never got easier. And yet his innards twisted and churned each time he looked.

With his work done for the moment, he stood and turned before heading out of the barn and securing the door. Before he drove away, he checked the boot for the shovel and gloves.

1

"Remind me again why we came here?" Abby asked. She checked the description online.

'*Lost in The Lanes*, a minimalistic café with a hip and vibey atmosphere. Perfect for the young, trendy, urbanites of Brighton.'

Abby stared at Scott and then back at her phone before returning her gaze to Scott again. "Since when were we classed as young, trendy urbanites looking for a hip and vibey atmosphere?" she added, raising a brow.

Scott batted away her sarcasm. "Listen, they do an awesome breakfast, toasted banana bread to die for, and apparently the best turmeric latte in Brighton. And I'm going to order all of it." He waved over a waitress.

The waitress took their order with a more than generous smile and dashed off with the energy and exuberance of a spring bunny.

"Turmeric latte? Really? Has hippy, earth-loving, planet-saving Helen got to you? Or am I sitting with Scott's twin brother I know nothing about?"

"This is all part of the new Scott. Since Cara fell pregnant, she's gone on a massive health drive. Brown rice, quinoa, a side salad with every meal, and a green smoothie every day."

Abby tossed her head back and laughed so loudly, other diners turned in curiosity. "Ah, it all makes sense now. You're having to eat whatever she eats at home. So you're stuffing your face with shit when she's not around." She narrowed her eyes and rubbed her hands together. "What's it worth for me to keep my mouth shut?"

He raised a brow. "Erm, your job!"

"Hell, I'd be happy to risk my job just to see the look on Cara's face. *If* I tell her."

Scott pointed an accusatory finger at her. "You're treading a fine line, Ms Trent. I'll do a deal with you. I'll pay every time we go out and eat, in return for your silence."

"Pay for all drinks and food in the canteen as well and you've got yourself a deal." She pretended to spit in her hand before extending it to Scott.

He pulled a face. "I'm about to eat. I don't want your spit all over me. But consider it a gentleman's agreement."

It felt good to have the old Abby back again. The last six to twelve months had been challenging for her. After Abby had finally walked away from her relationship with Jonathon, she appeared to be in a better place. Scott noticed how she appeared more upbeat and lighter in mood.

"How's the bump?" she asked, starting on her food.

"Not much of a bump at the moment. Apparently, it's the size of a peach. The baby I mean. Cara looks a little bloated. Anyone would think she's in the third trimester by the way she feels. Her legs hurt. Her back hurts. Indigestion keeps her up at night, and she's always hungry."

"Poor Cara."

Scott dropped his knife and fork on the plate and stared at Abby incredulously. "Poor Cara? Really? She's only in her first trimester. If she's like this now, what's it going to be like towards the end? I'm going up and down the stairs like a yo-yo in the middle of the night. I'm not getting much sleep, and I can't cook food quickly enough."

"Oh my God, listen to poor you. Anyone would think that you're carrying the baby with the way you're talking. I can tell she's not gonna get much sympathy from you through her pregnancy."

Scott laughed. "Hey, listen, I can be caring and attentive. And I will be. But she's milking this big time. She warned me about this when she fell pregnant."

"Well, you definitely need to grow out your fringe. Her thumbprint is going to get bigger by the month. Go along with everything she says or asks you for, and you'll be fine."

Scott finished his breakfast and wiped his mouth with his napkin before scrunching it up and throwing it at Abby. "What have I done in life to deserve this? Grief at home. Grief at work. Do you know arguing with women is like trying to read the 'Terms of Use' on a website? Eventually, you give up and say, 'I agree.'"

Abby rose from her chair and winked at Scott. "There you go. The penny finally drops."

2

Scott pulled up outside the address for Alison Chartwell, in a leafy suburban street in Hove. Alison had been a key witness to an armed robbery at a small newsagent a few days ago, where the owner had been threatened with a handgun before being pistol-whipped. Though the shopkeeper had survived, the trauma had subsequently led to him to put his business up for sale after twenty-five years in operation.

Abby rang the doorbell before scanning the clean, quiet and family-oriented street. The perfect location for growing families as it was close to the main road, within a short distance of local schools, and sought after by those living in Brighton who still wanted to be close to the action but preferred the quieter setting.

A middle-aged woman with a round face and a short bob answered the door. She held a young baby close to her chest.

"Alison Chartwell?" Abby asked.

The woman nodded and greeted them with a smile.

Abby introduced herself and Scott before the woman led

them through to the lounge. It was a warm and inviting room, with a few toys stacked in one corner, a baby rocker on the floor, and warm-coloured prints on the walls.

"I'm sorry about the mess, but we've got our hands full with this one at the moment, and a three-year-old. I only just got her off to sleep."

Abby smiled affectionately at the baby. "How old?"

"Seven weeks. Though it feels like she's been here for a year. I'm shattered."

Abby smirked at Scott as if to suggest *you've got this to come*. Scott stared straight ahead, unwilling to entertain her innocuous dig.

Scott mentally ran through the case file. Alison had been about to wheel her pram into the newsagent's when she heard the screaming and ensuing fight. The robber had pushed her out of the way as he fled. Though her baby was fine, she had fallen back and sustained some bruising to her back and elbow, which had left her shaken.

"How are you feeling now?" Abby asked.

Alison rocked her sleeping baby in her arms. "Pretty shaken up still. It keeps going through my mind. I can't imagine what would have happened if he had crashed into the pram and sent Amy flying. You don't think things like this are going to happen to you."

"I know. It can be quite a scary experience. And, thankfully, your baby was unharmed. We appreciate the witness statement you provided. The description that you gave us of the robber has helped us quite a lot."

Alison winced as she leaned on her left elbow and felt a stab of pain.

Sensing the mother's discomfort, Abby suggested to Scott that he hold the baby whilst she continued with her questions. Scott's eyes widened, but he breathed a sigh of relief when Alison declined the offer.

"We've got a few pictures that we'd like to show you and wondered if you might recognise any of the faces?" Abby asked.

Alison shrugged. "I'm happy to help. Though I only saw him for a moment. First, when he came charging towards us, and second, when he glanced back after I'd fallen."

"We appreciate that. However, I have to say you've got a very good eye for detail, because the description you gave us was very clear."

"Well, I wouldn't go as far as to say that, but I'm glad it's been of use to you."

Abby retrieved a brown envelope from her bag before taking a seat beside Alison. "We are treating this as a serious robbery because a handgun was involved. Regardless of whether it was an imitation firearm or real, the threat was there, as well as the intention. The quicker we get this individual off the street, the better for all of us."

Abby spent the next few minutes sifting through the stack of photos, taking a lengthy pause with each one whilst Alison studied them. She scrunched her nose up as Abby went through them, shaking her head at the pairs of beady eyes staring back at her.

Just as Abby was getting to the end of her pile, Alison gasped. "I think that's him. I remember he had a tattoo on his face, but until now, I couldn't remember where it was. It was two overlapping stars on his right cheekbone."

Abby smiled and reassured her as she turned the photograph to Scott. He rolled his eyes.

"How sure are you?" Abby asked.

Alison nodded and pulled in air through her teeth. "I wasn't so sure until I saw this picture. But that's definitely him. An icy shiver ran through me as soon as I saw that face. I didn't experience that feeling with any of the other pictures. Sorry."

"Hey, there's no need to be sorry. That's brilliant. This individual is known to us. We may need you to come in and do an identity parade... if you're willing?"

Alison shrunk back into her chair as her shoulders stiffened.

"It's okay. You don't have to if you don't want to," Abby said. "Let me reassure you that none of the individuals in the line-up would know that you're there."

"I don't know. I really don't."

Scott cleared his throat. "It's absolutely fine. There's no pressure for you to be involved any further. Do have a think about it. At the moment we might not even need a line-up. We need to apprehend the individual first and question him. If there's an admission, then we won't need your help." The suggestion seemed to placate the woman. "I think that's all we need for the moment. Your statement has been crucial. The fact you've been able to identify the suspect from our photographs makes our job a lot easier. We won't keep you any longer and will see ourselves out. Thank you so much for your time."

They walked back to the car.

"Martin Enright," Scott said. "I had a feeling it was going to be that scrote. What worries me is that he's ramped up the threat level, switching from his normal MO of using a knife to a handgun. Let's get back to the office and update the team. We need to reach out to all our contacts, find out if anyone has seen him."

"Mike's usually good for this. He's got a few good snouts," Abby replied. "So you didn't fancy holding the baby, then?"

"I swear my back got sweaty when you suggested that. I don't believe you sometimes." Scott fired her a look.

He drove off with the sound of Abby's laughter ringing in his ears.

3

After returning to the office, Scott instructed Abby to send a few officers out to the last known locations for the suspect. He also instructed Mike to tug on the collars of his snouts for any information on Martin Enright.

Scott sat down at his desk and fired up his computer. His to-do list appeared to be growing by the hour. This recent case would take up a considerable amount of his team's time. They were also completing the case files with their prosecution team for the Buckley College court appearance.

A pile of the morning's mail sat in one corner of his desk. He groaned as he leaned forward and pulled the stack of envelopes towards him. One by one, he opened them. A few circulars from the Police Federation. A letter informing him about which officers in his team were due to go on officer safety training in the coming weeks. Scott rolled his eyes. Though every officer across the country needed essential training, having officers out of circulation for one or two days added undue stress to the rest of the team.

The last envelope, a small, plain-white, padded Jiffy bag, piqued his interest. He looked at the postmark, Kent, then squeezed the bag, curious about the object inside. Perhaps a promotional key ring? No, he couldn't feel a fob.

He tore open one end and he peered inside before shaking its contents onto the table. There was something wrapped within bubble wrap. He peeled off the tape and unfolded the package. A silver ring fell out and rolled across his table. It came to a stop.

Scott's eyes widened in curiosity before the first tendrils of fear, shock and horror spread through his body. He leaned forward and picked up the ring before dropping it seconds later. He recoiled in his chair as the item rolled across the carpet.

Scott yelled at the top of his voice, a guttural roar that reverberated around his room.

The noise drew the attention of his officers, who rushed in, confused by the commotion. Abby pushed through and stood in the middle of Scott's office.

He sat there motionless; the colour drained from his face. He gripped his cheeks and his eyes welled up. With trembling lips, he succumbed to the violent tremors.

Abby raced to his side of the desk and grabbed him by the shoulders. "Scott, what's the matter? Talk to me. What's happened?" Her voice rose with each word.

More members of his team gathered in the doorway, exchanging glances of confusion.

Trapped in a vortex of grief and confusion, Scott clenched and unclenched his fists. Involuntary moans rumbled in his throat. The room spun as waves of nausea hit him. His eyes scanned the room, unable to focus.

"Scott, you're scaring us. Someone call for an ambulance. Who is a first-aider?" Abby shouted.

An officer pushed through the crowd. "I am." He crouched down beside Scott and placed two fingers on his wrist whilst silently counting his pulse.

Scott's eyes bulged as he stared at the ring on his desk. His teeth chattered as he nodded at it. "It's... it's... Tina's wedding ring."

Abby looked at the ring. "Was it stolen? Was someone returning it to you?" She clutched at straws as her mind raced with possibilities. With Scott making no sense whatsoever, she didn't know what to do. "Are you sure?"

Scott nodded and swallowed hard. "Check... the... date... inside!"

Not wishing to touch it, Abby used a pen to pick up the ring. She took a look at the inside of the band. She could just make out the words *Scott* and *Tina*, and their wedding date.

Abby gasped. "Scott... what's going on? Was it stolen?"

He shook his head violently, unable to string words together. Adrenaline coursed through his veins as his body buzzed and shook. He looked at Abby and then at the rest of his team.

A vacant expression crept into his eyes and settled there as tears escaped down his cheeks. "She was buried wearing the ring."

4

Panic spread as horrified officers stood around not knowing what to do. Mike stepped outside to call Meadows. Before long, the man came running along the corridor.

"Mind everyone, let me through," Meadows bellowed as he barged into Scott's office. It took a moment for Meadows to adjust to the melee as Abby tried to calm a hyperventilating Scott.

She got up and joined Meadows, then gave him a quick rundown of the situation and the significance of the ring. Concern etched Meadows's features. He turned over his shoulder and whispered something to one of the officers behind him, who scurried off.

"Oh my God, what happened to Tina? How did someone get hold of her ring?" Scott shouted, as he jumped from his seat.

Sweat beaded on his forehead. He grabbed hold of the side of the desk to steady himself as waves of nausea rushed over him again. He turned to one side and threw up on the carpet. Abby didn't jump back in time and puke sprayed her shoes. She grimaced and began to retch herself as the acidic smell of vomit filled the room.

"Calm down, Scott," Meadows said, as he tried to corral Scott back into his chair. "There must be a perfectly reasonable explanation for this." He regretted the words the moment they left his lips because his platitudes only inflamed Scott's reaction.

Scott glared at Meadows, rage twisting his features. "You're not listening to me. I buried Tina wearing that ring. There's no other way that anyone could have got to this ring unless they opened her coffin." Scott jumped from his seat and attempted to make his way to the door. "I need to get there. I need to know what's happened."

Meadows and Abby stood in Scott's way.

"Stay here, Scott. We've sent officers to check," Abby said, her voice gentle and reassuring. She rubbed his arm, trying to calm him. "You won't be doing yourself any favours if you go there. Let them report back to us first." She looked around at Meadows and the assembled officers. "Let me speak to the guv alone, please?"

Meadows furrowed his brow in protest at the idea, but Abby stood her ground.

"Please?"

Meadows nodded reluctantly then encouraged the rest of the officers to leave the room and wait in the hallway. He glanced back at Abby as if to say, "I hope you know what you're doing." Then he closed the door.

Scott looked at Abby, his eyes pleading. "I need to see what's happened to Tina."

"Scott, listen to me. We don't know what's going on yet. I'm really worried about you. Please, for your sake and mine, wait here until we hear back from the other officers. It won't be long."

"You don't understand. Tina was buried wearing this ring. There are no other rings. There is no other explanation. Someone has dug..." Scott shuddered, as tears squeezed from his eyes.

Abby pulled him close and held him tight, offering comfort as best she could in an untenable situation.

His eyes suddenly widened. Panic tore through him and the veins stood out on his neck. "Becky!" he shouted. "They're fucking dead if Becky's grave has been touched."

"Scott calm down. Please?" Abby begged.

He pushed her away. "I can't do this. I've got to go there." He jumped up from his chair and raced for the door. He flung it open and charged down the corridor, despite the protestations of Meadows and the other officers. A junior DC tried to grab Scott's arm. Scott violently tugged it away and glared at the DC, letting him know in no uncertain terms to back off.

"Mike, get up to the cemetery fast!" Abby shouted as she ran after Scott.

Scott clattered down the stairs three steps at a time. Officers that he passed looked on in consternation and confusion as he whizzed past them. Abby struggled to keep up; her heart thundered in her chest. She didn't know what she was doing or how she could help. She helplessly watched Scott plough ahead, making one reckless decision after another.

"Scott! Wait for me. Don't do this!" Abby shouted, chasing him across the station car park towards his car.

Scott fumbled for his keys, unable to clearly focus as tears blurred his vision. He was about to open the car door when Abby barged into him and pushed him aside.

"Give me the bloody car keys, Scott." He stared at her. "I mean it. If you drive away from here, I'll have you arrested for being unfit behind the wheel."

"Get out of my way, Abby. Please. Get out of my way."

She snatched the car keys and shoved him in the chest. "Fine. If you really want to do this to yourself, I'll drive you there my bloody self."

Abby drove the short distance to the cemetery with Scott silent and staring out the window. She showed her ID before the officer waved her through. Noticing the heightened police activity up ahead, she parked a short distance from an area of cordoned-off ground.

Scott flung open his door and raced off in the direction of Tina's grave, weaving around the various memorial stones, his expression a mask of grim determination.

"Stop him!" Abby shouted, pumping her legs as fast as her heart.

Officers heard Abby and two officers moved to block off Scott's path when he tried to dodge around them. "Guv, you don't want to see this. It's for your own good." They grappled with him when he put up a brave fight to shake off their interference.

"I need to see. Those are my wife's remains!" he shouted, as he tried to get around them.

"No you don't. This is as far as you can go. This is a crime scene," one of the officers replied, just as Abby finally caught up.

Scott continued to resist their efforts to contain him. He glanced over their shoulders towards a cordoned-off area where a pile of earth sat in a large heap, ready to fill a hole. But that hole had already been filled many years ago when he'd buried Tina.

He sank to his knees and let the uncontrollable sobs overtake him.

5

Officers stood in huddles, shocked and saddened. Many reflected in quiet contemplation at the vile and heinous act. It would have saddened even the hardest amongst them, but the fact it had been committed against one of their own only added to the depravity of the situation.

With Scott being held back for his own safety, Abby made her way over to Tina's grave. A solitary officer stood guard and acknowledged her with a nod. A large, blue tarpaulin covered the mound of earth and the remains of the desecrated plot.

"Is it as bad as I think it might be?" Abby asked.

The officer pursed his lips and nodded. "Yes, sarge," was all he could say before he looked away.

Every cell in her body willed her to walk away, but she needed to see for herself. She grabbed one corner of the tarp and pulled it back to see a crudely dug hole. Abby closed her eyes for a second before opening them and swallowing hard.

The darkened pit drew her in. Wet, slimy and cold.

Looking over her shoulder, Abby spotted Mike and Meadows making their way towards her. She pulled the cover back in place and joined them away from the plot.

"How bad is it?" Meadows asked, as he scanned the cemetery.

Abby sniffed loudly before clearing her throat. "Awful. The pit is partially submerged. They smashed open the lid of the coffin and..." Abby fell silent as she choked up.

"Have they interfered with the body?"

Abby shook her head. "Not that I could see. But I can confirm that she is missing her wedding band from her left hand. I don't know what to say to Scott."

Meadows sighed heavily. "Me neither. Becky's grave?"

"Untouched, sir."

Meadows blew out his cheeks in relief. "Mike, can you alert forensics? We need to gather any evidence from the scene."

Mike nodded before pulling out his phone and stepping away from them.

"Any ideas behind the motive?" Meadows asked, as he stood shoulder to shoulder with Abby staring at the blue tarpaulin.

"I really don't know, sir. I think we can rule this out as being a random desecration of a grave. This is personal. Never in all my years as a police officer have I seen anything like this."

Meadows agreed. "I've come across family members of officers being attacked. But this takes it to a whole new level. I need you to take Scott home and keep him away from here. Keep him under bloody lock and key if you have to. Tell Cara to keep a close eye on him. I'll swing by later."

"Understood, sir. What are you going to do?"

"I wish I knew. If it's personal, then Scott could be in danger as well. Assign an officer to be stationed outside his house until we know what we're dealing with."

"Will do, sir."

Meadows turned to Abby. "How are you after examining the scene?"

"Put it this way, sir. What I saw will haunt me for the rest of my life. Not because some nutter with a screw loose dug up a grave and exposed a dead body. But because *she* was Scott's wife. Scott was pretty messed up after he lost his family. I honestly think this could set him back and send him over the edge again."

Meadows understood. The entire force had pulled together to support Scott through his loss. He remembered visiting Scott on many occasions and seeing a rapid decline in Scott's health and wellbeing on each visit. He'd been inconsolable at the time and hadn't left the house for months. It had been touch and go whether Scott would return to the force.

The thought now crossed Meadows's mind that they may lose Scott forever this time.

6

Scott collapsed on his sofa and clasped his hands over his head, tucking in his elbows over his chest. He felt paralysed by hopelessness, guilt and dread. Worst-case scenarios flashed through his mind.

"Why, Abby? Why would someone do this?" he asked, pleading more than anything else.

She didn't have the answers.

Abby knelt down in front of him and rested her hands on his knees. She wanted to take his pain away, but knew that nothing she could say would help. "I don't know. I really don't. We need to make sure that you're okay. Cara is on her way and between the three of us we'll work out those answers."

Scott tugged at his hair. "None of this makes sense. What did I do? What *did* Tina do for some sicko to dig up her grave?"

"Scott, stop thinking like this. I'm as confused as you are. I can't begin to imagine how you're feeling. But I'm here for you. Cara is here for you. We are all here to support you in whichever way we can."

Abby's words appeared to have little impact on Scott's erratic behaviour as he continued to grimace and stare. A look of confusion spread across his face, as if the room was suddenly alien to him.

Abby heard keys being placed in the door and hurried off into the hallway.

Cara looked as if she had seen a ghost as she dropped her bag in the hallway and peeled off her coat. She placed a hand on her chest, trying to steady her breath. Her eyes widened as she searched Abby's face for answers. "Mike filled me in. I'm lost for words. How is he?"

She shook her head. "He's in a bad way. I've not seen him like this in a long, long time. It's knocked us all for six. I can't get my head around it."

Cara nodded. "You and me both. I don't know what to say to him."

Abby gave Cara a hug. "We all need to be there for him. We are still trying to understand the motive behind this."

Cara walked into the lounge and stood rooted to the spot, staring at the man she loved. He looked broken with those heavy, swollen eyes. He stared back at her like a lost child. She rushed to him and he stood up to meet her. She flung her arms around him at the precise moment that Scott burst out crying.

"It's okay, Scottie. I've got you. It's going to be okay. You're not alone," Cara whispered through her own tears.

Abby stood a few feet away wiping her own damp eyes, as a sense of helplessness washed over her. Scott had been there for her when she had been at her lowest. He had been her rock. His words had gotten her through her darkest moments, and yet here she was unable to say or do anything to ease his pain. She wondered if anyone could do that for him?

Cara sat Scott down and offered him a tissue. He blew his nose loudly and wiped his sore eyes. "Why would anyone do this?" he hissed through clenched teeth. Sadness and grief had momentarily switched to anger and frustration. He thumped a fist on his thigh.

"That's what your team is going to find out for you, Scottie. This is the most despicable of acts. I can't even begin to fathom what kind of depraved mind could do this."

"Me neither. But I'll fucking kill them. I'll..."

Cara held out a hand to stop him. "Scottie, I don't want you talking like that. At the moment, we need to come to terms with what's happened. Retribution, justice and all that kind of stuff can come later. We need to make sure that we support you and keep you in a good place, otherwise..." She couldn't bring herself to finish the sentence. The thought of losing Scott tightened her chest. It was as if someone had reached in and squeezed their hand around her heart.

"I'll make us a cuppa," Abby said, giving Scott and Cara some privacy.

7

Meadows arrived sometime later, and Abby met him at the door. There was a sombre atmosphere and a ghostly silence between them as he lingered in the hallway with Abby.

He then asked, "How is he holding up?"

"Not good, sir. He's in bits. I think anyone in this situation would be. It's come out of the blue and knocked us all for six."

Meadows nodded in agreement.

"Any news from the cemetery?" she asked.

"Matt's team is there. I've also assigned a search team to do a fingertip search of the area around the grave, and then a more extensive search across the grounds. I'm not confident that we'll find much. The grass has been trampled down around most of the graves, so it's going to be hard to determine where the perpetrator entered and exited. We do have boot impressions from around the grave."

Abby sighed. "Well, I guess that's better than nothing."

"Has he said anything else?" Meadows asked.

"Nothing that makes sense," Abby replied, leading him into the lounge.

Meadows's arrival went almost unnoticed by Scott as he stared at the floor, lost in thought. Cara offered the man a small smile before turning to Scott and tapping him on the knee.

Scott looked at Cara before turning his attention to their new visitor. "Why?"

"We don't know yet, Scott. There are a lot of questions that need to be asked. At the moment, we don't know if this was connected to you or to Tina. That's what our investigation needs to find out."

"I swear I'm going to find the bastard who did this. This person has crossed the line," Scott growled, as anger simmered beneath the surface.

"Scott, I'm putting you on compassionate leave. You are to stay at home whilst your team conduct this investigation. I'm placing Abby as the acting SIO."

Scott jumped to his feet and his clenched fists by his side.

"You can't do that." He jabbed a finger at his boss. "I need to track down the person who did this. Not you, not Abby, not the force. Me!"

Meadows stared down Scott's glare. "This is the precise reason you won't be leading the case. This is too personal for you to be objective. You are emotionally involved. And there's not a single force up and down the country that would allow a senior officer to be in charge of an investigation that affects them."

Meadows took a deep breath before continuing. "I know how much you're hurting, Scott. We may not have seen eye to eye over the years, and I'm sorry for that. But whoever did this has crossed a line. I want to catch this bastard as much as you do. But I don't want you impeding our investigation. When we catch them, and we *will* catch them, I don't want any bias or prejudice to influence our chances in court. That's why I want Abby running this case. She can give you an update every day, if necessary, but I need you out of the way."

Scott shook his head and stared at the others in the room, as a flash of anger prickled his skin. It felt as though they were all ganging up on him. He marched over to the drinks cabinet, pulled out a bottle of Jack Daniel's and reached for a glass. Cara raced over to him and grabbed him by the wrist.

"No, that's not the way to deal with it. Please." Cara released her grip and wrapped a hand around his waist. She stared into his eyes and pleaded silently.

"She's right, Scott," Meadows added. "I know you've hit the bottle in the past. Don't think it went unnoticed. I let it slide at the time because of what you went through. I won't let you do that again."

"I need *one* drink. Just one!" Scott fumed.

Cara pushed him away from the drinks cabinet. "That one drink leads to another, then another, and then another... I will not let you do that. You can hate me for that but I don't care. I care for you and want to look after you. We all do."

Meadows let the situation calm down and took the chair opposite Scott. "We'll be looking at this from lots of angles. Starting with you. Can you think of anyone who may have wanted to get back at you? A personal or professional grudge?"

Scott shrugged. "How long have you got? Everyone we arrest and charge wants to kill us, rape our partners, follow our kids home from school, stalk us, and seek revenge."

Meadows knew the truth in those words because it came with the territory. Nearly every person arrested and charged from a drunkard on a Saturday night to a murderer would throw out death threats. The list was endless.

"I appreciate that. That's something we're going to have to work through. Is there anyone in particular you can think of whose threats felt plausible and that you took seriously?"

Scott searched through his memories. He shrugged. "I don't know. I need to think about it. I've visited Tina's grave so many times. It's always been a special place for me. Now this has happened. I'm not sure I can go back there again. It feels violated."

The four of them sat in silence for a few moments.

Scott rose and bolted for the hallway. "I need to see Becky's grave for myself."

Meadows and Abby raced after him. Just as Scott made a grab for the front door, Abby pulled him back. Meadows stepped in between him and the door.

"Scott, her final resting place is fine. Becky... is... safe."

8

Abby gathered the team together around her desk. Officers moved in silence, taking a seat where possible. There was none of the usual frivolity, banter or jokes. Absent were the treats normally on offer, courtesy of Raj. The mood in the office was just as dark as the one at Scott's place.

Abby took a moment to scan the faces, seeing a mix of sadness, shock and concern etched in their features. She knew they felt the same pain as her.

"Okay, team. This is really difficult for all of us. You've all seen the body cam footage. To recap, someone ransacked the grave of Tina Baker in the early hours of this morning. They smashed her coffin open and though Tina's body is intact, her wedding ring was removed."

"How's the guv holding up?" an officer asked.

Abby took a long, deep breath before replying. "I wish I could say he was holding up well, but I would be lying. This is so far left field that I still think he's finding it hard to process what's happened. I'm finding it hard. I can only imagine how it's affecting him."

Several of the officers nodded in agreement.

"The boss has put me in charge as the acting SIO. We need to work together to find out who has done this and bring them to justice. There is very little to go on so far. An envelope, postmarked from Kent, is with Matt's team at the moment. We need to begin by looking at any known contacts in the Kent area connected to the guv."

Officers made notes as Abby briefed them.

"We've got footprints from the scene. Forensic officers are making impressions. Judging from the photographs I've seen, they are fairly large."

Another officer chipped in. "I'm not being sexist, but with the amount of soil removed and the force needed to break through a lid of a coffin, it would be unlikely a female could do that on her own unless others were involved as well."

"Possibly," Abby said. "For the moment we work on the assumption it might be male or female, and there may have been more than one person involved."

"Any CCTV?" Raj asked.

"Only at the front gates. They were closed overnight. So whoever did this gained access some other way. I'm heading back to the scene straight after this briefing to have a proper look around." Abby turned to the whiteboard and added a few notes before continuing. "We need to check Tina's background, family, work associates. The lot. Who did she mix with? Had she fallen out with anyone? As much as we don't want to entertain the idea, are there any disgruntled ex-lovers that we are unaware of?"

A female officer held up her pen to catch Abby's attention. "How can we be certain it's about Tina? I'm thinking it could be about Tina or the guv?"

"Absolutely. I think it's a process of elimination. We start with Tina first and see what gets thrown up. The guv was married to Tina long before many of the officers here knew him. Personally speaking, I never heard a bad word uttered against Tina in all the time I've known her."

Abby assigned several officers to trawl through all the cases where Scott had been an SIO in the past five years. She also added they were to extend the time frame to ten years if nothing popped up.

Raj chipped in next. "I'll check with prisoner releases over the last couple of years. It might help us narrow the field."

Abby agreed and gave Raj the thumbs up. "I've also spoken to the guv. He can't think of anyone who might have a grudge and would go to these lengths for revenge. He wasn't thinking clearly when I left him. I do plan to sit down with him again and probe him further."

"Hold on a minute," a DC called Claire interrupted. "What about the case about four years ago where we put away the boss of the OCG? What's his name?" she said, clicking her fingers trying to remember.

"Jack Dempsey," another officer replied.

Claire's eyes lit up. "That's the one. Do you remember a couple of other members from the OCG were based in Spain and threatened to get to Scott when he least expected it? I know they were hiding out in Spain, but they may have slipped back into the country? Or they had other members of the OCG do their dirty work for them? We didn't get all of them. I remember he sent an envelope to the guv with a six-inch nail in it *after* he got sent down."

Abby pursed her lips and thought about it. The syndicate Dempsey put together was a slick and a well-oiled machine. Two-thousand-pound encrypted phones using EncroChat to stop police forces tapping into their conversations; clandestine meetings on yachts moored off the wealthy playground of Puerto Banús; an army of fifteen- and sixteen-year-olds running county lines, and well-paid yacht owners who ran shipping routes between Belgium and Ireland. Dempsey had a fierce and formidable reputation, and his signature punishment was hammering six-inch nails into his victims' kneecaps using a club hammer.

"Dempsey screamed across the courtroom after sentencing that the guv was a dead man walking. Perhaps he couldn't get to the guv directly, but *got at him* in different ways?" Claire added.

"Mike, can you work with Claire on that angle? I want to know every visitor Dempsey has had since being banged up. Every letter received, every phone call he's made, and what all his top lieutenants are doing. Which ones are enjoying life at Her Majesty's pleasure, and which ones got away? Also, cross-check for any connections to Kent." Abby dismissed the team after her final instructions and grabbed her bag and keys.

9

A bby's skin prickled as a shiver snaked down her back. Unease at being back here again left her feeling uncomfortable. She couldn't tell if the temperature had dropped a few degrees or whether the shock and fear from her first visit had returned. She saw the blue forensic tent erected over Tina's grave. And though she tried hard to forget, her mind kept pulling her back to that morbid sight. Images flashed of the broken casket and Tina's body.

She made her way over towards the scene, but something inside stopped her from getting there. It was as if her body and subconscious mind were in cahoots together, protecting her from what she'd seen.

Seeing her approach, Matt ducked under the tape and made his way towards her. "Hey you. You okay?"

Abby shook her head. "I know cemeteries are supposed to be tranquil, offering the perfect last resting place for loved ones. A place where families can visit the ones they have lost and still feel connected to them. But this is the last place I want to be at the moment." Abby stomped her feet on the spot. "This doesn't feel serene or tranquil. It feels like the worst nightmare for anyone."

Matt nodded and agreed. "Spare a thought for my team. It's probably the most challenging job they've been called out to. How's Scott?"

"I don't know, but he was in a pretty bad way when I left him earlier today. I'm trying to give him and Cara some space. I'll stop by there tomorrow morning on the way to work. How are we getting on here?"

"We haven't got much to go on to be honest. We've taken photographs and clay impressions of the footprints. There's nothing else there. No discarded tools, items of clothing, or even hair fragments. They are literally going over the area around the grave inch by inch, on their hands and knees."

"And they've found *nothing*?" Abby paused for a moment as she realised how that might have come across. She grabbed Matt's arm. "Sorry. I didn't mean it to come out that way. I'm not doubting your team."

"Hey, I know. We're all a little on edge and frazzled. We are desperate to crack this," Matt replied, looking over his shoulder towards the tent.

"I've got an officer stationed by Becky's grave. We'll have a police presence there twenty-four hours a day in case someone comes back to ransack her grave. Exhuming Tina's grave is one thing, but doing it to a child... I can't let that happen."

"Good shout," Matt replied.

Abby left Matt to get on with his work after the grounds manager, Ronnie Townsend, met them. She took the opportunity to walk around the perimeter with him. He was a middle-aged man, rotund, ruddy face, with messy hair tucked under a baseball cap.

"Awful business... just awful. I'm still trying to get my head around what's happened," he said with a shake of his head.

"We all are," Abby replied, as Townsend led her around the cemetery, sticking to the perimeter. "How easy is it for someone to get in here unnoticed?"

"Certainly not along this bit." Townsend pointed. "This boundary wall backs onto the gardens of properties on Hartington Road. We back onto allotments at the far end, so I guess someone could come through there."

"And Bear Road?"

"Low-level brick wall along the full length. Not hard to scale if you want to. You could easily hop over and disappear into all the trees and go unnoticed."

"You don't make it hard for trespassers, do you?"

"Well, everyone in here is dead. And there isn't much to steal..." Townsend trailed off when he realised what he had said.

Abby shot him a glance, surprised at how easy it was for him to talk of the dead in such a casual manner. "So it's going to be impossible for us to determine which route the perpetrator took?"

Townsend shrugged. "Pretty much."

It wasn't the news that Abby wanted to hear. "Only CCTV is by the main entrance?"

Townsend nodded and cleared his throat, not wishing to repeat his flippant remark again.

"Okay, Mr Townsend. Thanks for showing me around. It's thrown up more questions than answers unfortunately, but that's not your fault. I'm going to arrange for officers to do door-to-door enquiries along Bear Road. You never know, someone might have seen something suspicious or have CCTV pointing out towards the road."

Townsend tipped his cap before heading back to his office.

Abby checked her phone, finding no new updates or messages. With the evening creeping in and the first signs of darkness, there was little else she could do here. As much as she wanted to head back to the office to keep working on the case for Scott's sake, she needed to get home to her kids. Helen and Raj would cover the late shift. She fired off a text to both of them before jumping back in her car and heading home.

10

The look on Cara's face told Abby everything she needed to know about things at home. Cara stood in the doorway pinching the skin on her throat. She looked at Abby through a watery gaze.

She stepped through and gave Cara a hug. They embraced for what felt like a few minutes, each offering one another comfort and reassurance.

Cara took a step back and wiped her eyes before offering Abby a weak smile. "Thanks for coming."

"Try keeping me away. You look exhausted. Did either of you get much sleep last night?"

Cara shook her head. "A few minutes here and there. After the initial shock it's really hitting him hard. I'm worried about Scott. This isn't good for him."

"It's not good for you either. The stress that you guys are under at the moment isn't good for you or the baby."

Tears snaked down Cara's cheeks, which set off Abby.

Cara whispered, "I don't know what to do. Everything I

say falls on deaf ears. I know he's in shock but it's like I don't exist..."

"I know. But we both have to be strong for Scott. He's only recently come to accept that they are gone. You had a big part to play in that. You brought happiness back into his life. And he may not realise it at the moment, but he really needs you. We have to keep trying to get through to him... Agreed?" Abby grabbed Cara's hands.

Cara sniffed loudly and smiled weakly, responding with a small nod before leading her into the lounge.

Abby squeezed Cara's arm. "The boss is arranging for a specialist support officer to get in touch. We have an in-house counselling service. They're better trained at handling officers who've been through traumatic events."

Abby held her breath when she saw Scott. He looked a wreck. A lack of sleep and not having shaved, along with crumpled clothes, made him look like shit. She knelt next to him and rested her hand on his knee. She gave it a soft rub. Scott's eyes remained fixed on the wall opposite.

"Scott, look at me. It's me, Abby, that pain in the arse person. We are both worried." She glanced up at Cara, who stood there biting the nail on her thumb. Crease lines formed on her forehead.

Abby was lost for words. She had never seen Scott like this before – a shell of his former self. She had to find a way through his grief to reach the capable man and officer he was.

"Scott, I'm not leaving here until you look me in the eyes. We have been through so much together. And there's no way on this planet I'm letting you slip away." She squeezed his knee. "You were there every time I hit rock bottom. And you never abandoned me. Even when I tried to push you away or shut you out, you were like a bad smell that never went away. You kept coming back at me. Now it's my turn to do the same."

The room fell silent.

"I'm on my way back into the office. I promise you we are doing everything we can to find out who has done this and why. Every single officer in CID is on the case. We want to do this for you... and your family. I know this isn't gonna be easy for you. Meadows doesn't want you on the case, but I promise to update you on every single shred of information that we get."

Abby's mouth ran dry as she ran out of things to say, to fill the empty silence.

Scott's lips parted a fraction. He broke his stare and looked down at her. "Tina didn't deserve this." His lips hardly moved.

Abby glanced at Cara, whose eyes were wide in a mixture of surprise and relief.

Abby turned back to Scott and smiled softly. "No, she didn't. Neither did you. I'm going to the office now."

She stood and took a few steps back to allow Cara to move in and sit alongside Scott.

Cara wrapped her arm around his shoulder and with her free hand, entwined her fingers in his. "She's right. Once you've had the opportunity to freshen up, it might clear your head and make you feel better."

Scott turned his head to Cara and squeezed her fingers. "I'm sorry. I never wanted you to see me like this. I'm just... shocked. Appalled. What kind of a monster does something like this?"

"Shhh. Please don't apologise. Let's talk about this after you've had a shower and freshened up, hey?"

Scott nodded before getting to his feet and leaving the room.

"Thanks for coming over," Cara said, hugging Abby. "Keep in touch."

"I sure will."

11

Abby took a few moments to update the team on her visit to Scott. They clearly found her account both disturbing and upsetting. Several officers wiped away tears, whilst others shook their heads in anger and disgust. Meadows joined the quick briefing, keen to be involved as much as possible.

"I know it's upsetting, and we all want to catch the bastard. Sorry, sir," Abby said.

Meadows nodded and encouraged her to continue.

"It is unlikely that we'll get much evidence from the cemetery. Matt's team are working diligently but, following my visit this morning, he didn't appear hopeful about having any significant forensic breakthroughs." She turned to a whiteboard and pinned up an aerial map of the cemetery. "I also took the opportunity to look around, and as you can see from the map" – Abby ran her finger along Hartington Road – "at least half of the boundary backs onto residential homes. The chances of us knowing which way the perpetrator entered are slim."

Abby instructed Helen to organise enough bodies to begin door-to-door enquiries and recover copies of any CCTV footage covering the few hours before the call came in.

"Have we got any indication yet as to the motive?" an officer asked.

Abby shrugged. "None whatsoever. Scott wasn't able to shed any light on the motive. At the moment we're completely in the dark. Where are we with our initial enquiries?"

Another officer raised a hand. "I've been looking into Tina's background. There's nothing on the system around any reported threats. I spoke to members of her family. She had no connections to anyone in Kent."

"Any problems with former partners?"

"Again, her family said she only had one other serious boyfriend, David Templeton, before she met the DI. He currently lives in Scotland with a wife and two kids. They run a hotel together." The officer searched his notes. "I spoke to David first thing this morning. He wasn't even aware that she had been killed in an RTC. That knocked the wind out of him. He sounded quite shocked on the phone to be honest. He had nothing but nice things to say about her."

"And the reason they split up?" Abby probed.

"They drifted apart. They were incompatible. He said they ended on good terms."

"Okay, thanks. Anything else?"

Claire piped up next. "Mike and I have been looking at the Dempsey angle. He's currently in Long Lartin, serving time as a Cat A. We've already put in a request with the governor for a copy of the visitor logs, any phone calls he made, and who he hangs about with on his wing."

"Excellent. Claire, can you get back on to the governor and ask his officers to turn over Dempsey's cell and do a search? We're looking for any mobiles which might have given him the opportunity to talk to someone on the outside. If he's connected in any way, then he could have given instructions to others."

"That's if he is still in possession of a phone when they shake him down," Mike said. "They are good at moving phones around the wing. That's why it's so hard to find and confiscate them. A phone could swap hands half a dozen times a day. We might get lucky, but then again…"

Abby agreed with Mike's observations. However, she knew they had to try. If Dempsey was involved, then it made sense to let him know they were paying close attention to his movements.

"Mike, can you do me a favour and get onto the local force? Explain what's happened and ask them to have a chat with Dempsey. If they notice anything that might be of interest, then I'll send our officers up to have a chat with him. As it stands, I want to limit resources being tied up on a wild goose chase. We need everybody here."

Abby wrapped up the briefing as Meadows joined her.

"Well done, Abby. You handled yourself very well. I'm yet to go back and see Scott, but it sounds like he needs every ounce of support we can offer him."

"Yes, sir. Thanks. I agree. But I also think a lot of our officers need that support as well. It's incredibly difficult for all of us."

Meadows nodded. "Well, my door is always open if you need to talk."

"Thank you, sir," Abby replied, as she headed off to Scott's office.

12

I t felt odd sitting at Scott's desk, but as SIO, she wanted to adopt the attitude and mindset that Scott would expect of her. Away from the crowded floor, it gave her time to think. She tapped her credentials into the computer and searched the case file on the tragic accident involving Becky and Tina.

Abby drew a gasp of breath when she clicked on the photographs associated with the scene. Her mind darted between the image of Tina's body in her desecrated grave and the photographs taken by crime scene officers of her mangled and twisted remains in the middle of Western Road. At first Abby couldn't bring herself to move through the photographs, but knew she had to as she viewed the crime scene images of Becky's tiny body.

Abby shook her head. It angered her that the culprit or culprits hadn't been brought to justice. Though the burnt-out remains of the car had been discovered not long after on a dirt road near Devil's Dyke and the Brighton and Hove

Golf Club, forensics hadn't been able to gather any useful evidence from the twisted metal remains of the BMW.

Abby read through the witness accounts.

I heard an almighty thud and scream, though I can't be certain which one came first. I just remember looking around and seeing two bodies fly through the air. I'll never forget the sickening thud as they hit the ground. It wasn't until a few seconds had passed that I realised one of the bodies was that of a little girl. She flew through the air like a toy doll.

She skimmed another witness account.

I'll never forget the screams. Everyone stood there frozen to the spot for what felt like ages, paralysed with shock. Then it just went crazy. People were running to the victims. I'll never forget the crying faces of passers-by as they knelt around that poor, little baby girl.

Abby's mind conjured up ghastly images of the scene. They played out in her mind as if she'd been there.

It happened so quickly. They didn't stand a bloody chance. Whoever did this was just utterly despicable.

As Abby leaned back in the chair, her eyes settled on that last word. The report couldn't confirm the driver's identity. A lack of CCTV had hampered the progress of the investigation. A CCTV camera on Western Road near the Preston Street end was out of order. A further trawl of camera footage had captured the car on North Street and then again on Preston Road before it had disappeared for good.

Abby wondered if the incidents were connected. She pondered. Both had to be? They were extreme and violent events, and in her opinion, targeted. But her thoughts returned to one simple word: Why? What had Tina done for such vile acts to be committed against her?

Abby rocked back and forth in the chair as more questions surfaced. What if both events were not connected? What if they had been committed by different individuals for different reasons? Was this really about Tina? Or was it connected to Scott?

Abby blew out her cheeks and took a breather. She then turned her attention to a few envelopes sitting in Scott's in-tray on his desk.

She gave each envelope a cursory glance, but froze when she saw one. Another Jiffy bag. Kent postmark. Lumpy. Object inside.

Abby dropped the envelope on the table and rooted through Scott's desk for some gloves. She snapped on a pair of latex ones before slowly peeling the Jiffy bag open.

Peeking inside, she saw four A4 sheets of paper folded in half, and a memory stick. As she unfolded the sheets, her eyes widened.

She dropped them on the table in shock, and jerked her head back.

"What the fuck?"

13

After Abby's call, Matt and Meadows raced down to Scott's office and charged through the open door.

"Same person you reckon?" Meadows asked, as he came around to Abby's side of the desk.

She nodded. "I think so. Identical-looking Jiffy bag. Kent postmark. I've kept it clean."

Matt leaned in and took a closer look. "I'm not having much luck with the other envelope. It's got a few partial prints on it, but I'm not sure whether they belong to the sender or the posties. If my hunch is right, then we won't get much from this envelope either."

Abby had left the sheets of paper where she'd dropped them, but spread them out so the other two could see them. A solitary picture of Tina filled each sheet. Each picture was different. "It looks like they were taken from Tina's Facebook page and printed off with a standard inkjet printer."

Though the pictures were a little grainy, each one showed Tina posing for the camera. Her brilliant-white smile jumped out of each shot, showing her in happier times. In the first one, she sat at an open restaurant by a beach, which Abby assumed was somewhere on holiday. In another, she held a striking pose at the foot of some elegant stairs. The two other shots had been taken of her in a packed pub.

"I don't understand this," Abby said.

"Me neither," Meadows replied. "What's on the memory stick?"

"I don't know, didn't get that far. I thought I'd wait until you got here." She passed the stick to Matt who'd brought one of his laptops with him following Abby's request.

She and Meadows waited patiently, still staring at the images of Tina, whilst Matt did a security and virus scan on the stick.

"It's clean. There is only one file. An MP3. It's an audio file."

Meadows headed to the door and closed it before nodding at Matt.

A muffled voice broke through the laptop speakers.

"It hurts to lose someone, doesn't it? You're probably pulling out your hair trying to make some sense of this. Is it about you? Or is it about someone else? I've got some bad news for you."

Though the file continued playing, there was a lengthy silence. The three of them exchanged glances of confusion and curiosity. Then the muffled voice continued, breaking the oppressive silence in the room.

"Let's talk about your wife and daughter. It was a tragic accident, wasn't it? Bet it hurt like hell, right? So much that you went out of your mind. It must have destroyed you knowing the car dragged your daughter along. You spent endless nights questioning why? You were filled with anger, especially when they found the car burnt out. Justice wasn't served, was it?"

"Is there a point to this recording?" Meadows muttered, as his impatience grew.

"Justice wasn't served for you... but it was for me. That hit-and-run wasn't an accident. It was deliberate. I did it. I needed to see justice for everything I lost. You fucked me up so badly that I wanted to do the same to you. You turned me into this monster. My life changed and so did yours. How does it feel knowing you are responsible for their deaths? Not me... you!"

The voice had risen in such loudness and aggression that the last three words were spat out. Abby blinked hard as her mind spun in confusion.

The muffled voice continued. *"I'm coming for you. I'm going to fuck you up beyond all recognition. I've just proved that I can screw you without laying a finger on you. It must have hurt like hell to know that whilst you thought your rotting, dead wife was safe, resting in peace, I was staring at her."*

At hearing the icy, menacing and vicious voice, a prickle of fear stabbed Abby, as if a thousand needles were jabbing her skin.

"You took away my happiness. I'm about to take away yours."

The recording stopped. Matt and Meadows stared in silence at the laptop. Abby simply blinked. She pushed back the chair and rested her elbows on her knees. She covered her face with her hands.

"This can't be happening. I don't understand this. The bloke sounds like a complete psycho," she muttered through her hands.

After a lengthy and uncomfortable pause, Meadows spoke up. "Matt, I want that recording analysed with a fine-tooth comb. Any background noises? Any unusual noises? The intonation of his voice? Any hints of a regional dialect? I know it was muffled to disguise his voice, but this recording is the only lead that we have to the person who's done this."

"Consider it done. I know someone at the lab who specialises in voice recognition and analysis. If anyone can pick apart this tape, she can."

"Do it, Matt. Throw everything you've got at this. Sod the cost. I'm also going to authorise an armed presence to be stationed outside Scott's house day and night until this is sorted. I want this scum caught."

Abby got up and grabbed her coat. "Great idea, sir. I'm going to Scott's. He needs to see this, and I promised that I'd update him on every single new development."

"Abby, I'm not sure that's wise," Meadows said.

"I appreciate what you're saying, sir, and I will tread lightly. But this investigation has taken on a whole new turn. This isn't about Tina as we thought. This is about Scott."

14

Cara met Abby at the door. During her drive over, Abby had phoned Cara about the new information, and now as they stood face to face, concern creased Cara's features.

"How is he since I saw him this morning?" Abby asked as she loitered in the doorway.

Cara let out a sigh. "He's better. Having a shower and shave helped to shake him from his mood, but he's still pretty cut up."

She led Abby through to the kitchen and joined Scott at the dining table. Cupping his mug of coffee, he offered her a weak smile.

"It's good to see you looking fresh," Abby said, leaning over and rubbing his arm.

Scott nodded. "It helped a bit. My head feels so foggy. I don't know whether to laugh, cry, or scream. I don't understand why anyone would do this."

"We've all been struggling with it." Abby pulled an envelope from her bag and placed it on the table. "I promised I'd come and see you as the case progressed. There's been a development."

Scott looked up from his coffee cup and stared at Abby, his face taut.

He had been in such a mess when she had visited earlier that it pained her to heap even more sadness and confusion on his shoulders. He looked so much better than the dishevelled, tired mess she had seen this morning.

"Because of what happened at Tina's grave, we initially believed the attack may have been directly linked to her. We've been picking apart her background to see if it uncovered anything."

Scott's eyes narrowed as he leaned forward in his chair.

"We received another envelope today with information that suggests that the attacks on Tina were directly linked to you."

"Wait... attacks? What do you mean? Her grave was wrecked once..." Scott questioned.

Abby removed the pages from the envelope. "These are photocopies of what we received today. These are images taken from Tina's Facebook page. I guess from before it was taken down."

Scott looked through them, his eyes darting from one image to another. His lips parted as if to say something, but nothing came out. Cara sat beside him, saying nothing as she stared at the images then at Abby.

"I don't get it. Why would he send you pictures of Tina?" Scott mumbled.

"There was a USB stick with a voice recording on it. The perp said that you destroyed his life and so he wanted to destroy yours in return. He said he's coming for you." Abby continued to relay the main points of the message. As she did, Scott shook his head in disbelief.

"Listen, Scott, there's more." Abby let out a deep breath. "There's something really important and there isn't an easy way to say this. The individual on the tape claims to have been the person who mowed down Tina and Becky on Weston Road. He said it wasn't an accident, but deliberate. He was getting back at you for destroying his life."

Scott took in a sharp breath and his body stiffened. He shot a look between Abby and Cara before returning his gaze to the pictures of Tina.

Shaking his head, he jumped to his feet.

"No. No! This is a wind-up. Why?" Rage coursed through his veins. His skin flushed, as he raced towards the kitchen door. He slammed a fist into the wood. A growl tore from his throat and his eyes bulged with fury.

Cara leapt up and tried to calm Scott when he began pacing around the room.

Abby remained seated, struggling with her emotions. It was the last thing she'd wanted to say to Scott and knew how much it would hurt. But he needed to know. "That's what we are trying to find out. We need to determine if it's a credible threat as well as if this guy was involved or not. He could have used information in the public domain and may not have been involved in the hit-and-run."

Cara guided Scott back to his seat.

Abby asked, "Scott, can you think of anyone you've come across in your career who made such determined threats against you that you believed them?"

"No. I can't think of anyone."

"Scott, think. I really need you to work with me on this. This isn't about Tina, it's about you. They're trying to get back at you. Can you think of any cases where a suspect, or even a victim, lost someone really close to them? A parent? A husband?"

As Cara squeezed his arm in silent support, his body ached from the emotional pain that gripped his heart. But he had to think hard, despite the confusion clouding his mind. He had to help Abby.

With a ragged sigh, he met her gaze. "I honestly can't think of anything off the top of my head. We get death threats all the time. It's part of the job. But if we took each one seriously, we wouldn't get far in our careers."

Abby knew that her questioning was going nowhere. In Scott's current state, he wasn't thinking straight. Her news that an armed presence was being authorised to watch the house only added further tension.

She rose from her seat. "If you think of anything, then let me know. I'm heading back to the office now. I'm going to get the team to do a thorough review of your background. Maybe a fresh set of eyes will help us to find something. You get some rest and I'll speak to you soon."

Abby closed the front door behind her and let out a heavy sigh. Her mind swirled with the thoughts bouncing around inside it. The gravity of the situation wasn't lost on her when she walked down the garden path and saw a blue unmarked BMW X5 series pull up outside the house. The plain-clothes officers inside nodded at Abby as she passed.

15

"How did he take it?" Meadows asked, as he caught up with Abby near Scott's office.

Abby shook her head and rolled her eyes, visibly shaken after her visit. "Not good, sir. He looked a lot better than when I saw him this morning. At least he had tidied himself up, but the news of the photos hit him badly. He went ballistic."

"Do you blame him?"

Abby shook her head, closed her eyes, and rubbed her temples.

Meadows folded his arms and glanced up and down the corridor. He leaned in to Abby. "Was he able to shed any light on a motive?"

"I'm afraid not. He's so overwhelmed that he's finding it hard to process even the simplest of thoughts."

Meadows tapped a finger on his chin, as he thought through the case. "We must be looking at a convicted suspect. Someone who lost his freedom and livelihood... Though I hardly consider a life of criminality a *livelihood*.

Perhaps he lost his family after being sent down. The fact the man on the recording talks about how Scott took away everything including his happiness makes me think more than his freedom was stolen."

Abby agreed. She was leaning towards that theory too. They were used to getting hate mail and death threats. This was something more sinister. Abby promised to update Meadows as soon as she knew more. They headed in opposite directions.

The noise across the CID floor was louder than normal. It appeared as if every available officer was on the phone or tapping away on a keyboard. Abby noticed officers huddled around a few desks, swapping information and trying to piece each morsel of information together.

Raj was busy on the phone, so Abby made her way over to Mike's desk where Helen was perched on one edge. Abby took a moment to update the pair on her visit to Scott. Both appeared visibly upset. They fell silent and stared off into space for a few moments.

Mike broke the silence. "I can't believe this. I swear if I find the bastard, I'll use him for target practice on the range."

"Get in line behind me," Abby said. "Not only are we trying to track down this lunatic and find out why he's on a path of revenge but, and this is between the three of us, Meadows has placed a plain-clothed, armed response unit outside the DI's house, because we believe there is a serious threat to his life now."

Helen's eyes widened. "Shit."

Abby nodded in agreement. "How are we getting on with tracking down any leads?"

Mike leaned forward and wiggled his mouse to bring up a list. "We've been going through all the cases the guv has been the SIO on for the last five years. These are the ones that ended in a conviction and custodial sentence."

Abby leaned in and placed her hands on the desk, to take a better look. "Any death threats?"

"Plenty. The usual bollocks. 'I'm going to fucking kill you.' 'You will pay for this.' 'You've messed with the wrong person.' That kind of shit."

"Normally I would agree with you there, Mike. Water off a duck's back. This time we have to take each threat seriously. Any of these," Abby said, running her finger down the screen, "could have snapped. They could still be in prison and have connections on the outside to carry out their orders, or they've been released and are out for revenge."

"We've crossed-reference those names," Helen chipped in. "We are looking for any extenuating circumstances. Subsequent loss of family members, their house, money, or anything like that. I'm also looking at bank records for each of these individuals. The bank balances could have been frozen if it was identified that the money held within them was from the proceeds of crime. There is one name in particular that I've spotted so far that has a red flag for me."

Abby was impressed with Helen's thoroughness. She asked her to cross-reference known associates on the outside with any of those who were still incarcerated. "Has anyone on that list been released early? Let's say in the last few weeks or months?"

Mike scanned the list and searched out the name that Helen was referring to. "Vince Swann. He was released five months ago. A nasty toerag. High propensity for physical violence. A charge list as long as your arm. Hates the police, so nothing new there."

Abby stared at Swann's picture while Mike pulled up his

records on the screen. Abby raised a brow. It appeared as if Swann had spent most of his life in the gym. A tank of a man with biceps as thick as tree trunks, and a chest that barely squeezed into a T-shirt. Small and menacing eyes glared back at her. He reminded Abby of the murderer Raoul Moat. Her colleagues in the Northumbria Police had chased and tracked Moat down after he had shot dead a person and then shot and critically wounded two others, including a police officer.

"You wouldn't want to meet him in a dark alley, would you?" Mike said, as if reading Abby's thoughts.

"He's bloody enormous. What's the red flag with him?" Abby asked, running a hand through her hair and stifling a yawn.

"Brothers Vince and Ken Swann were involved in a gangland feud. I remember the case. It's going back a few years. Scott was involved in a car chase. We were trying to apprehend the pair. Vince was driving and Ken was in the passenger seat. Vince lost control and stacked it." Mike scrolled down to review the notes on the system. "Ken was thrown clear as the car rolled but he suffered fatal injuries. Vince swore that when he got out that he would make Scott pay. They removed him from the dock kicking and screaming."

Abby stared at Swann's mugshot again. "I think we need a word with him."

16

A bby stepped from her car and checked the address one more time. She made her way to the door with Mike following behind. A sensible precaution in her eyes, considering the man-mountain they were about to see. Abby had also called for uniformed backup to be positioned close by, just in case.

Due to the warm May weather, more people were out and about. She glanced around and spotted neighbours across the road chatting over garden fences. They were so engrossed in a conversation that they hadn't even seen Abby pull up and make her way to the property. Flowers were in bloom and the smell of freshly cut grass lingered in the air. The distant hum of a lawnmower and the sound of a bleeping alert from a reversing Sainsbury's delivery van added to the subtle busyness.

"Ready?" Abby asked, as she glanced back at Mike. He gave her the thumbs up in reply.

She rang the doorbell and waited a few moments. A

silhouette appeared in the frosted glass. A small woman with grey hair opened the door and peeked through the gap.

"Hello? Can I help you, luv?" she asked. Her voice was soft and pleasant enough.

Abby held up her warrant card. "I'm Detective Sergeant Abby Trent from Brighton CID. This is my colleague, Detective Constable Mike Wilson. We are looking for Vince Swann. May we come in for a moment?"

The woman rolled her eyes and opened the door. She stood there, hands on her hips. She wore a long cardigan. It hung down to above her knees. "What's Vince done this time?"

Abby shrugged. "Nothing as far as we are aware. We wanted to ask a few questions."

"I'm Fran, his gran. Come in, luv." She ushered Abby and Mike into the kitchen and offered them a seat. "Let me put the kettle on."

Abby held up her hand in thanks. "It's fine. We don't want to put you to any bother and won't be long. We need a quick word with him."

Fran waved away Abby's words. "Don't be silly. I give everyone who comes here a cup of tea and a slice of cake. It doesn't matter whether you're a copper, the vicar, or a plumber. I was always taught that you can tell a lot by a person's manners. When I grew up, we didn't have a lot, but that never stopped my mum welcoming everyone who stepped through our door."

Abby glanced around the kitchen. Everything looked old and worn. The plates, kettle, and even the table mats looked as if they would fit in nicely into one of the antique shops in The Lanes.

Abby glanced at Mike. He rolled his eyes as if to suggest, "We could be here some time."

"Does Vince stay with you?"

Fran nodded enthusiastically. "Whenever he can, sergeant. That's of course when he's not banged up inside." She smiled at Abby. "That's not a dig at you or the police by the way. I know you're only doing your job. And rightly so. Vince and his... brother." Fran sniffed and stared at the kettle a moment before continuing. "Well, they're not the easiest of boys. Fell in with the wrong crowd when they were much younger. My daughter, Carol, died of cancer many years ago. So they came to live with me. They're a right handful."

"And their dad?"

"Carol's husband worked at Shoreham docks. He's dead too."

Fran didn't elaborate how, and Abby wasn't interested in finding out either. "Is Vince around?"

"He is, luv. I've sent him out to the shops for me. I can't get about as much as I used to. He should be back any minute now."

Fran picked up a tray with three cups of tea and a plate with slices of cake. Worried by the slight tremble as Fran shuffled across the kitchen floor, Abby took the tray from her and set it down.

Mike didn't need to be invited. He reached across and helped himself to a slice of cake.

Fran smiled and winked at him. "A big boy like you needs feeding. You are just like my Vince. And you, sergeant, you need a bit of fattening up. Nothing that a bit of liver, kidneys, mash and gravy, washed down with a pint of Guinness, wouldn't solve. I've got some faggots in the fridge if you want some?"

Abby raised a brow in reply and smiled politely. *Liver. I can't think of anything worse. Kidneys? Offal? I think I'm going to throw up.*

Mike bit into the cake and chewed. He paused and glanced at Abby, as his face twisted and his lips tightened.

"How are you liking my pineapple cake? My mum passed down that recipe," Fran bellowed proudly.

Mike with his lips clamped tight and reluctantly murmured his approval. Abby hid a smile behind her hand.

"Well, get that down your gob and have another slice," Fran said, pushing the plate towards him. "I have some nice raspberry jelly cakes and Battenberg slices you can have as well."

17

"Have you been here long?" Abby asked, checking the time on her phone. This wasn't turning out the way she had expected. Now they were making small talk with Vince's cake-making gran.

Fran took a sip from her tea and nodded. "All my life. Elsie and Albert, my parents, lived on the Whitehawk. I was born in '46, not long after my dad came back from serving his country. He had a lot of catching up to do with my mum and I came along less than a year after he returned. He clearly couldn't wait to drop his trousers. Mum said he was always waving it around. Dirty sod! Need I say more?"

Abby cleared her throat and pushed away the images invading her mind.

"A lot has changed since then. It was a great place growing up. Mind you, I heard a lot of stuff about how difficult it was back then. Back in the fifties, there were a lot of men who were unemployed for nine or ten years. If they didn't pay the rent, the landlord would take away the front door or the windows. We only had as much furniture as we could carry on a handcart, and I remember one time not even having a blanket on our bed. We used my dad's overcoat."

The picture Fran painted reflected a different bygone era. But Abby couldn't help noticing how Fran spoke about it so affectionately.

"Sometimes we were lent blankets by the Ebenezer Chapel in wintertime. Then my mum would wash them by hand and return them in the spring. It was a lot different back then. We looked out for one another. People who lived here stayed here. Ted the milkman delivered around the valley for years. Everyone knew him. Even Cracknell the veg man would go around the valley with his horse and cart on his grocery round."

Fran stared off into the distance and smiled, as her memories took her back to pleasant times. "Not much changed in the sixties and seventies. I never thought twice about leaving my front door open and popping next door for a natter with my neighbour and being gone hours. Kids would be up and down the street on their bikes. Or playing football over at the green. They'd be on and off those swings and slides all day long. All the mums would have a nightmare trying to call their kids in for dinner."

Fran chuckled to herself. "Summer of '68. The battlefield scenes for *Oh! What a Lovely War?* were filmed on the corporation tip on Wilson Avenue. Plenty of kids made a fortune collecting the empty beer bottles used by the actors and crew and returning them to the Whitehawk Inn. They also sprayed artificial snow all over the tip. It was amazing."

"It sounds like a lovely place. A real community atmosphere," Abby replied.

Fran nodded and smiled. "It was. And still is. Yes, we

have a few bad apples, but everyone around here is as good as gold. Proper working-class people who value a sense of community and respect." Fran wagged a finger at Abby. "I wouldn't think twice about putting some of these young shits over my knee and giving them a smacked arse for being naughty."

Abby didn't doubt Fran's grit and sense of respectability.

The conversation stopped when the front door opened. Mike placed his cup down and pushed back in his chair so that he faced the kitchen door. Abby stiffened when she saw the imposing Vince Swann stride through the hallway and fill the doorway to the kitchen. He looked as if he had the strength and size to dig up a grave.

He glared at the visitors and then at Fran. Abby clearly saw that Vince wasn't as pleased with his house guests as Fran was.

"Who are you?" he growled out.

Abby held up a warrant card and introduced herself and Mike.

Swann stepped around them and placed the bag on the kitchen counter before reaching down and giving Fran a peck on the cheek. "I got all your bits, Gran. I also picked up a chocolate Swiss roll because I know you like them." Swann didn't take his eyes off Abby and Mike.

"Bless you, you're a good boy. You spoil me too much. These two lovely officers popped in because they wanted a word with you. We've just been having a lovely time reminiscing about what it was like growing up on the estate. Shall I pour you a cup of tea?"

Swann shook his head and clenched his teeth. The muscles in his jaw flexed as he stared at Mike and Abby. "No, I'm okay, Gran. What can I help you with?"

Abby glanced at Fran before looking back at Swann.

Swann tutted. "Whatever you need to ask you can say in front of my gran. We haven't got any secrets."

"Okay, Vince. There's been an incident involving one of our senior officers. During your court case and subsequent sentencing you made threats towards Detective Inspector Scott Baker before you were taken away. Does that ring a bell?"

Swann growled. "Of course it does. He killed my brother and put me away."

"Where were you the night before last?"

"Here, looking after my gran. She doesn't like being left alone at night."

Fran nodded silently.

"Do you own a laptop or a printer?" Abby asked.

"No. Why?"

"Just asking. Do you mind if we have a look around?"

Swann pulled his shoulders back and straightened up. "As a matter of fact, I do. This is my gran's house. If you want to search it, come back with a search warrant."

"I assume you own a mobile phone?" Abby continued.

"I do. And no, you can't look at that either."

No. But we can request your phone records, you shit.

"We may need to speak to you again, Vince. We understand that the case involving you and your brother sadly resulted in his death. And the threats that you made towards Detective Inspector Baker are now being investigated by our team. We'll be conducting further enquiries in the meantime."

Swann sniggered. "You've just turned up here on a fishing trip and caught nothing. If you came round here to tug my chain, then you've had a wasted trip. If you had anything concrete on me, you would have dragged me down to the station by now. Whatever has happened to your inspector has nothing to do with me. What I said, I said in the heat of the moment."

"Exactly," Fran chipped in. "You lovely officers were doing your job. Vince did wrong and he was punished for it. We all say things that we later regret when we calm down. He'd just lost his brother. He regrets making those threats, don't you?"

Swann smiled. "As Gran said, after I'd calmed down, I regretted saying those things. And I definitely regretted making *those* threats."

Abby examined Swann. He sounded sincere, but that sincerity didn't reach his eyes which bore into Abby.

"Thank you both for your time and hospitality," Abby said. "It's been helpful. We'll see ourselves out."

"Well, luv, if you're both in the area again, my door is always open. If you feel a bit parched and fancy a cuppa, you know where to come." Fran remained seated while Swann escorted the officers to the door and out.

Abby paused halfway down the garden path and looked back at Swann. He stood there glowering at them.

"We'll be in touch," she said.

Swann sneered. "If you turn up here again, make sure it's with a search warrant and ten officers, because you will need that many to get past the doorway if I have anything to do with it."

18

He slid out of bed and stood in his darkened room. A few flecks of light wormed their way through gaps in the curtains. There was a heavy silence.

Pain spread through his jaw when he clenched his teeth tighter. A desire for vengeance rippled through his body. He wanted to hurt someone. He wanted to see blood. Doctors had mentioned the word cathartic when they had suggested grief counselling. In his mind only one thing would be cathartic, and that would be to inflict the very same pain he had experienced onto others.

Every morning was the same. It started with a gnawing pain in his head that refused to go away. He would slap the sides of his skull begging to be free then stare up at the ceiling. There was never anything up there. Emptiness. Darkness. A reflection of what he felt inside. It had been this way for over a year now. He didn't want to talk to anyone. He regularly avoided making eye contact with people and when anyone came knocking on the door, he would plug his ears with his fingers.

Was there any point in living? He'd asked himself that question every day for over a year. The same answer came back. No. Despite wanting to leave this cruel world, he needed others to feel his pain first.

He lay there fighting for breath; it felt like someone was kneeling on his chest. It felt like a hand had been plunged deep inside his belly, reached up to his heart, and ripped it from its warm protective space before pulling it out.

All their shared personal items were gone. Keeping them only tormented him further, so he'd boxed them up and donated them to charity shops. He had thrown himself into various projects to avoid dealing with the pain that tortured him. Each room in the house had been decorated several times in the space of a year. A feeble attempt to erase the past.

On the odd occasion he went for a walk, it was at night, to avoid others. For some strange reason he was drawn to graveyards. In the stillness of the night his mind could be at peace, as he rubbed shoulders with the spirits. Sometimes he would sit and sob as he read the heartfelt tributes set in stone. At other times, he felt more at home with the dead than he did with the living. They couldn't harm him.

A profound loneliness had crept into his life over the last year. His mind would tilt from moments of deep sadness to rage. He'd suddenly explode over seemingly little things. This morning felt no different as an invisible force pushed and shoved him.

Fuelled with anger, he hissed, "I'll kill you!"

Turning to his new parcel, he ripped it open and ran his fingers over the fine black cloth of the shirt. His eyes fixed on the garment and all that it stood for. It meant nothing to him, though it would for millions of others. This was merely a means to an end.

A shiver of delicious anticipation ran through him when he considered raising the stakes. He knew he couldn't get near Scott. A walk in the early hours of the morning had confirmed that. He'd seen two men sitting in a car outside his house. He would need to get to the detective in a different way. And he could.

Today was the day that Scott would never forget.

19

"How are you feeling this morning, Scottie?" Cara asked, as she placed a cup of tea on the bedside table.

Scott had the covers tucked under his chin. His eyes flickered open and he let out a slow breath. "Like I've been hit by a bus." He instantly regretted the analogy and choice of words.

Cara stroked his face and combed her fingers through his hair. "I know. I can't imagine what you're going through at the moment. Just remember you're not alone. You've got me. Don't bottle anything up. Keep talking to me. Okay?"

Scott's eyes settled on Cara, but he didn't even have the energy to muster up a weak smile.

"Shall I take a cup of tea out to the boys?"

"No. They'll have officers on rotation. More importantly, they need to maintain a discreet presence. They can't be connected with this house."

Cara nodded. "I'm going to pop out to the shops to get a few bits. Is there anything you need?"

"I don't think that's a good idea. The police are out there for my protection... and yours. They can't do that if you're not here."

Cara offered him a small smile. "I know. I'm literally just going to the nearest corner store. We need a few bits for the fridge. Then I'm going to the office to grab some files. I've got someone covering my work at the moment, so that all the post-mortems we've got booked in can continue. However, I have some reports that I need to finish. I thought it would make sense to bring them back here. At least I can still be near you and get on with work."

"Why don't you just get a delivery organised?"

"I can do, but it won't take long. And besides, I'd still need to go to the office anyway. I promise I'll be back before you know it."

Scott reminded Cara to keep her phone on and fully charged with the location tracking on.

Touched by his concern, she reassured him she was a big girl and could look after herself.

"I'm really not comfortable about you going," Scott added, as he pulled himself up in bed.

"Listen, it's broad daylight. It's busy out there and I'm going to be inside a shop surrounded by lots of others. I'm perfectly fine and safe."

Cara leaned in and kissed him softly then studied his features. It looked like he'd aged ten years in just the space of a few days. Dark, heavy bags hung beneath his eyes. The white clarity of his eyes looked yellow, peppered with red lines, and his jowls sagged. She spotted the deep-red and purple bruising on his knuckles from when he'd punched the door.

"I'll phone you when I'm at the shops and then again

when I'm at the office. I'll also phone you as I'm heading back. How's that?"

"You can be a right stubborn cow when you want to be," Scott murmured, as he took a sip from his tea.

"That's why you love me." She winked. "Let me shoot off now. The quicker I head off, the quicker I'll get back. I don't want to leave you a minute longer than I need to. Are you going to be okay?"

Scott nodded and yawned. "I think I'll feel better once I have a shower and a shave. Abby's popping in with an update. Don't be long."

"I promise."

20

C ara turned off the Lewes Road and into a narrow turning. She cruised down the street, tapping on the steering wheel, whilst looking for a space to squeeze in and park. Most of the roads leading off this part of Lewes Road provided cheap shared accommodation for university students. The houses were small and terraced, and the road was too tight for two cars to pass. A short walk to the university, and an abundance of fast-food shops with a scattering of cheap supermarkets, made it popular with students.

Cara left her car in a parking bay and rushed back towards the main road. Darting into the local Co-op, she scooted around the aisles picking up a few essentials. She made her way to the dessert section and picked out some treats, hoping to cheer up Scott.

Selfishly, she welcomed the opportunity to get some breathing space from everything going on back home. Time away would let her mind settle. Moving through the store, she paused every so often to check her phone.

No messages from Scott. Phew.

It meant there weren't any further developments and by now Abby should be there to keep him company.

Cara made her way to the self-checkout and scanned her items before making her way back to the car.

Vehicles moved slowly through the sheer volume of traffic on the busy road. It was one of the major routes in and out of Brighton and was always active. Students scurried towards a campus, heads down, earphones in, oblivious to the world around them. She'd always liked this part of Brighton. It was close to her work, and she often wandered up and down this stretch when taking a breather. She marvelled at the eclectic mix of shops. Cheap takeaways sat shoulder to shoulder with quirky second-hand shops. A plethora of estate agents had sprouted up over the years to serve the growing number of private landlords who'd flooded the area and snapped up cheap property, to cash in on digs for students.

Cara pulled out her phone and dialled Scott's mobile number. He picked up within the first few rings.

"Cara, is everything okay?"

"Scottie, I'm absolutely fine. I said I would call you. I'm heading back to the car. Next stop is my office, and I will call you when I'm leaving."

"Okay. I'm not comfortable with you being out. I can't protect you if you're not near me."

Cara smiled. Scott always thought of others first. Even through the pain of the last few days, he was still thinking of her foremost.

"Scottie, please don't worry. I'll be home in a flash. Call you soon."

21

C ara hung up and grabbed her keys from her coat
pocket. Up ahead, a man was walking the pavement slowly staring at the house numbers. He
held a small package.

*A delivery driver. Why today? Why does a man have to be
standing between me and my car when Scott's worried about me
getting back?*

As her heartbeat accelerated, Cara looked up and down
the road. Two students were leaving a house at the far end,
but they were too far away for her to shout and get their
attention. They glanced at her for a second before turning
and heading towards the Lewes Road.

The delivery man took a step forward, as if to ring on a
doorbell. As she passed, the man spun on his heels and
shoved Cara with force towards the open side door of a van.
Before she could call for help she stumbled, her legs giving
way as her shins crashed against the metal sill, stopping her
from going any farther. Spreading her hands to cushion the

impact, she fell into the cargo space and landed on her face. A scream tore from her throat.

Her body folded as a moan escaped her lips. She grasped at the floor to try to regain control. She wanted to call for help but couldn't. The air had been pushed from her lungs and shards of pain spiked through her body.

The man jumped on her back and slammed the side door shut. She panicked and tried to get up. He grabbed her flailing arms before securing them with a cable tie.

"Shut up or I'll kill you right here," he hissed, as he rummaged through her handbag. Her attacker pulled out Cara's phone and ripped off the back before pulling out the battery and SIM card. She knew he'd toss them along the way.

Desperate to hold onto a source of stability and awareness, Cara's eyes darted around the darkened space, absorbing everything in her environment. Waves of nausea hit her stomach as she fought for breath, due to the crushing weight on her back.

She heard the tearing of tape and a piece was put over her mouth. Then everything went dark when her assailant threw an old blanket over her. Cara wriggled and rolled over onto her side. She gained instant relief when the pain in her chest subsided. Her body trembled as she retreated into the foetal position, her muscles tense, her skin clammy.

The van started up and pulled away, sending her body sliding across the floor. Confusion clouded her mind. Dread filled her thoughts.

Will I ever see Scott again?

22

"I come bearing gifts," Abby said, holding up a Costa coffee bag.

Scott offered her a weak smile as he let her in and gave her a warm hug. He was in no hurry to let go. Abby rubbed his back.

"Thanks, I needed that hug," he said, leading her into the kitchen. It was nice to feel a sense of normality and Abby was great at settling him when he needed it the most.

"How are you holding up?"

Scott shrugged as he planted his hands on the kitchen worktop. "I don't know if I'm coming or going. It feels so alien to be sitting around on my arse. I want to be back in the office leading this investigation."

"I know. We'd love you back, but you are under orders. Besides, I get a chance to treat you for a change. Coffee and a Danish?" she said, pulling two drinks and pastries from the bag.

"You know how to spoil a man."

"Well, you need to keep your strength up. At least you don't look like shit today. Where's Cara?"

Scott filled her in as he took a sip of his coffee. "Ah, that tastes good. She should be back pretty soon. Are you going to wait for her?"

Abby nodded.

Scott stared at his coffee.

"We will get to the bottom of this..." Abby tapped him on the back of the hand. "I mean it. We've got every single person on this case. Everyone is going above and beyond, even Meadows, and that's because of you. We all care about you."

"Thanks. It means a lot. I'd feel a lot better behind my desk. I hate sitting around. What's happening with the investigation?"

Abby began by going through the various threads of the investigation, elaborating on certain elements when Scott wanted to know more.

"Do you remember Vince Swann? Gangland feud. Car chase. Brother, Kevin, lost his life?"

Scott raised a brow as he searched his memory. "Yep. I do now. What's the connection?"

"We're not sure at the moment. When he got sent down, he swore revenge for the loss of his brother. He was released five months ago. We paid him a visit, but we got more from his lovely gran than we did from Swann."

Scott shook his head. "It takes an extreme psycho to dig up a grave. Can we place him in that category?"

"I don't know if I'm honest. We are looking at all his known associates and his phone records."

"I don't think it's him. He wasn't on our radar for anything, and we hadn't crossed paths before Tina and

Becky lost their lives. He came along after. You need to be looking elsewhere."

Abby sat up straighter and studied Scott's features. The lightness in his face had been replaced by pain again. "We've another person of interest. Jack Dempsey."

"Dempsey. I remember him well. How could I forget after receiving a six-inch nail in the post? What have you found out?"

"At our request, the local force had a chat with him. He denied everything and said if he wanted to get to you, he could have done so ages ago. Dempsey insinuated he had officers in his pocket. Whether or not that's true is a different matter." Abby tutted in disgust. "The bastard laughed in the faces of the officers who attended."

"Who has he been speaking to?"

"We're looking into that at the moment and checking every single name in the visitors' log. All his top lieutenants are still banged up bar one. The location of the individual is unknown." Abby paused for a moment and took another sip of her coffee before she continued. "We put in a request to have Dempsey's cell turned over. We didn't find anything."

Scott sighed. It was wishful thinking on his part that all the pieces of the jigsaw would come together quickly. He listened intently as Abby continued with her feedback. He couldn't find fault in the way she was conducting the investigation. The team were leaving no stone unturned. They'd contacted the sorting office in Kent that had postmarked the envelopes. Working back from there, they had pinpointed the whole geographical area that the sorting office served, including the location of every post box. They, in turn, had been cross-referenced against the addresses of any known associates of Dempsey's OCG.

"Abby, I appreciate everything you and the team are doing. At least you're getting a flavour of what it's like to be an acting DI and SIO." He laughed.

"Sod that. I would much rather be a DS any day. Less stress. The constant need to update senior management is doing my head in. But on this occasion, because it's you, I was happy to step up. Besides, I wouldn't have it any other way. You're a good boss, and an even better friend. It pains me to see you this way."

Scott slumped in a chair. "I've certainly had better days. I don't understand why. What have I done to hurt someone so badly?"

Abby shrugged. She didn't have the answers that Scott needed.

23

The van skidded to a halt. Silence prevailed for a few moments then Cara heard the driver's door open and slam shut. She shivered with fear. Darkness caused by the blanket shielded her. In a perverse way she felt protected, but her mind raced.

Why did he take me? What is he going to do with me? How can I reach Scott?

The side door slid open and bounced against the rubber stoppers. The man tore away the blanket and tossed it to one side. Cara remained curled, her knees tucked into her chest. Light from beyond the van caused her eyes to sting. She blinked hard, forcing herself to focus.

Her abductor stepped inside the cramped space. She flinched as he placed a black hood over her head before dragging her from the van by her ankles. He grabbed her by her coat and pulled her upright; her legs gave way as she stumbled. Looping his arm through one of hers, he guided her away. Cara didn't know where she was going but felt long grass beneath her shoes that licked at her ankles. She listened for sounds, anything that could give her a clue, but all she heard was her laboured breathing.

She heard keys jangling and what sounded like a padlock being unlocked and doors being opened. They didn't sound like metal doors to her. *Perhaps they're wood? A shed?* And then she was moving again, being led by the arm. The texture beneath her feet changed from soft grass to something much more solid. *Stone? Concrete?*

He stopped her and then held her by each of her arms. "Sit," he whispered, as he guided her back.

She stumbled and fell hard into a chair. He cut the restraints and secured her wrists again to the sides of the chair, repeating the process to tie her ankles to the chair legs. Pulling away her hood, he admired his handiwork. He stepped to the right, and then to the left, before returning to his original spot and removing the tape from her mouth.

Cara winced as dry skin tore from her lips. She blinked. Her mouth fell open as her surroundings came into focus. An old wooden barn of some sorts.

"Please don't hurt me," she said in a shaky voice. "Why are you doing this?"

The man raised a hand to silence her. "You'll find out soon enough."

Cara's eyes widened as she looked down at the chair and then above her. Chains attached to the chair rose upwards to the roof, connected to a pulley system which disappeared into the darkness. Her eyes widened when she looked over her shoulder and saw a large, clear drum. It was huge. Perhaps ten feet high and just as wide. She'd seen nothing like it. Tendrils of fear snaked down her spine as she shivered.

"Please! You could let me go now. I promise I won't say

anything. Please?"

Cara's pleas fell on deaf ears. The man placed his hands on his hips and nodded appreciatively, as if still bowled over by his own efforts. He turned and disappeared over her shoulder. The rattling of chains broke the uneasy silence. Cara twisted from left to right, desperate to see what was happening, and then her worst fears left her paralysed with terror. The chair rose and the chains rattled louder. A scream tore from her throat and her chest heaved and tightened. Her vision swam when the chair rocked in the air. It was moving towards the opening of the tank. She screamed louder and sobs rattled her body.

Her mind exploded into full meltdown, unable to comprehend the hell playing out in front of her. The chair descended inside the bowels of the tank. It landed with a heavy thud and a few moments later, the man appeared in front of her on the other side. He stared through the Perspex, his features expressionless. She continued to plead and scream, begging him not to do this.

"Scream as much as you want. No one is going to hear you. You're miles from anywhere."

He walked off towards an improvised table made of upturned beer crates, where he'd set up a laptop and camera. He pressed a few buttons before returning.

"I'll be watching you. I'll hear every cry, every scream, and every plea."

Her kidnapper returned to the doorway and threw her a final look before closing the door and securing the padlock.

Cara's chilling screams faded into the distance. He put the key in the ignition, started the van, and drove off to the next location.

Rinse and repeat.

24

M ike pushed back in his chair and locked his fingers behind his head. "It's like looking for a needle in a haystack. There are so many cases, and everyone seems to have a grudge to bear."

Helen nodded as she closed another file and clicked on the next one on her list. "I know, Mike. We still need to keep looking. The last thing we want is to overlook one particular case and find that it's the one we needed to focus on."

"Yeah, yeah. I know. We see enough of these scrotes on a day-to-day basis. To keep going back over historical cases just pisses me off even further. Do you know what I find quite surprising? How many of them are out already. All they have to do is turn up, get banged up in a cell, and be a good boy. Before you know it, they have a third of their sentence taken off for good behaviour. Where's the justice in that?" Mike fumed.

"Mate, if we keep focusing on that we'll get nothing done. Besides, that's not what we're here to dwell on."

Mike and Helen carried on in silence for the next hour,

sifting through one case file after another. The task was already laborious but having to cross-reference each case with the prisoners' release list only dragged out the process.

Helen paused for a moment and leaned into her computer. Her eyes narrowed as she scanned the details. She clicked on a few pages and nodded to herself. "Mike, I think I might have something here. I found another case linked to the guv way back when he was a DS."

Mike popped his head above his monitor and chewed the end of his pen. "Go on."

Helen raised a finger as she double-checked the details. "Nick Newman. We arrested him for armed robbery. It turned into a bit of a shitshow when officers turned up with an arrest warrant. It all kicked off. He was arrested late at night in front of his kids."

"If you are looking for any sympathy from me, you will not get any."

"Hold your horses, Mike. The incident report highlights that Newman flipped his lid, and needed to be restrained by several officers when he tried to say goodbye to his kids. But that wasn't the issue. He was trying to whisper something to his wife at the same time."

Mike rolled his eyes as if he'd heard the story a thousand times.

"He blamed the guv for tearing his family apart and traumatising his kids." Helen continued to scan the reports and relay certain points to Mike. She was particularly concerned when, during his subsequent interview, he made threats to kill.

"Well, I don't think we've got time to look into that one. Some other muppet can check it out. It doesn't send any alarm bells ringing for me." Mike stood up from his desk and shouted across to Raj. "Raj, we've got a case you need to look into. Helen can ping the details over to you. I don't think it's a runner, but better to be safe than sorry. Is that okay with you, mate?"

Raj was in discussions with a support officer and signalled as if to suggest, "Yep, send the details over to me."

One of the post room staff loitered amongst the desks with a pile of post. Barely out of his teens, the lad looked lost going from one desk to another, asking who he needed to leave the bundle with. He was eventually pointed at Mike.

Shifting nervously on the spot, he cleared his throat to get Mike's attention.

"Something up?" Mike asked.

"Yeah. I've got this post. I was told to give it to DS Abby Trent, but she's not here. Shall I leave it on her desk or...?"

"No. Give it to me. I'm not sure what time the DS will be in. I'll go through it myself."

Relieved, the young lad turned on his heels and disappeared faster than a greyhound scooting around the track.

Mike took a hefty glug from his now cold coffee and rubbed his eyes. He could do with a break from scanning endless computer files.

He decided to open up a few of the envelopes. None were marked private or confidential, so he assumed it would be okay to continue separating those of importance from the junk. He'd worked his way through half of the pile before realising this was as boring as the task beforehand.

A white A4 envelope addressed to Detective Inspector Scott Baker was next on the pile. He checked the postmark. It wasn't from Kent but along the coast at Hastings. He ran his finger along the top and opened it.

The first picture stopped him dead in his tracks. He

quickly shuffled through the rest, his mouth widening in confusion and shock. "Fuck!"

Helen bobbed her head up. "What?" Her look of concern matched Mike's stiffened features. "What is it?"

Already up, Mike grabbed his jacket from the back of his chair. "It's another one!"

25

Less than an hour after opening the envelope, Mike hammered on Scott's door. Out of breath and stressed, his impatience grew as each second passed. He hammered again and cursed under his breath.

Abby finally answered, having received a text message from Mike that he was en route. She met his eyes and saw fear. "How bad?"

"I think we're in serious trouble," he replied, breezing past Abby in search of Scott.

"Mike, has there been a development?" Scott asked, as he jumped up from his chair.

Mike nodded as he opened the envelope and pulled out photocopies of the images they had received. Before racing from the station, he'd taken the envelope straight to Matt who'd secured the photos in an evidence bag.

Scott's eyes widened as he flicked through the images. His breath caught in his throat as his heart raced, his eyes widening in disbelief. Perhaps this was a joke? A wind-up?

He looked at Mike and then Abby. "No! No!" He threw

down the images and reached for his mobile phone, just as the realisation hit him square in the chest.

Abby came to the kitchen table and looked for herself at the covert photographs taken of Scott and Cara together. The date stamps alarmed Abby. The images had been taken over the course of a year. The first was of Scott's first date with Cara at the Chilli Pickle restaurant. Further images showed the pair together on Palace Pier playing on the arcade machines. Each new picture sent shivers of panic through Abby.

Shopping together at Sainsbury's. The Tempest Inn. Woolfies. Browsing The Lanes and darting in and out of curiosity shops. Another showed Scott running along Brighton seafront.

Abby's eyes widened when she saw a picture of Cara walking to Scott's front door. He was here, right outside! Every aspect of Scott and Cara's life together had been captured by a stalker... a killer.

"Shit," Abby whispered to Mike. Mike nodded.

"Cara, call me back when you get this message. It's urgent," Scott said.

Scott hung up and pushed past Abby. He raced for the front door, grabbing his jacket from the coat stand. "I can't stand around and wait for her to call. Her life might be in danger and she doesn't even know it. And it's my fault."

Abby followed, grabbed him by the arm, and spun him round. "Scott, don't do this. None of this is your fault. Okay? None of it. We're dealing with someone who's unhinged. We'll find her... together."

"I can put in a request with the team to get an immediate ping on her location. I don't suppose you've got the Track My Phone app on your phone?"

Scott nodded. He thumbed through a few apps until he found the right one. He closed his eyes and dropped his head in frustration. "It's not picking up her phone."

Mike came up the rear. "Where was she heading to?"

Scott ran a hand through his hair, racking his brain for answers. "The morgue. She was heading there to pick up paperwork and was supposed to call me when she was leaving."

Mike barged past Scott and Abby. "That's where we'll start."

26

Mike tore through the streets of Brighton, his tyres barely touching the road as he threw his car around the corners. Traffic swerved hard when they heard the approaching sirens and saw the blue grille lights.

Abby called ahead and asked for uniformed backup to meet them at the morgue.

"Fuck, fuck," Scott said, repeatedly punching the dashboard in frustration.

"We are minutes away, guv," Mike replied, tugging on the wheel.

He pulled into the morgue and screeched to a halt, abandoning his car in front of the doorway. The three of them raced to the door and hammered on the buzzer until one of Cara's technicians arrived, looking flustered and alarmed at the commotion.

Scott stormed in demanding, "Where's Cara?"

The female tech froze like a rabbit caught in headlights,

overwhelmed by the sudden intrusion. "Erm, I don't know. She's not here at the moment as far as I'm aware."

Scott raced through the building towards her office, shouting Cara's name.

"Has she been here today at all?" Abby asked, following in Scott's wake.

"No. We weren't expecting her in."

"Shit," Abby murmured. She caught up with Scott stood at Cara's door, trying her again on his mobile.

"Cara, it's me again. Where are you?" He stared pleadingly at the screen, as if doing so would magically make her call.

"Scott, I've put in a request with the team to get an immediate ping on her location," Abby said.

Scott shook his head in despair.

"Think. Where else was she going?" Abby pushed.

Scott paced around the office. "I don't know. She said she was popping to the shops."

"Which ones? Did she mention any in particular?"

He shrugged. "I can't... I don't... Where, um...?" he muttered in confusion, as he dropped into Cara's chair and buried his face in his hands.

"It could be anywhere between your house and here." As soon as the words left her lips, Abby realised how insensitive she sounded. "Scott, did Cara prefer to pop into any particular shops? Have you ever heard her mention any? What things did you like to eat?"

Scott lowered his hands after a lengthy pause. "Co-op... She loved going there. They have this cake thing that we both love. She said she wanted to cheer me up and would get me a treat. Maybe there?"

"Great, let's head there first."

Minutes later, the three of them were holed up in the Co-op manager's office trawling through CCTV for the morning. Scott scanned the footage on one screen whilst Abby and Mike reviewed footage from other vantage points around the store on a different screen.

"There!" Mike shouted, jabbing the screen. They crowded around the monitor and saw Cara dipping into an aisle whilst scanning the shelves. A sense of mild relief washed over them. At least now they had a firm sighting of her and a timestamp.

"Can we flip to the camera outside?" Scott asked.

The manager obliged and pulled up the relevant track. They watched in silence as Cara exited the store. She paused for a few moments looking up and down the road, as if deciding what to do next, before crossing over and disappearing from view.

"Shit," Scott hissed. "Is there a wider angle?" He looked at the manager. A solemn shake of the man's head offered little relief. "Abby, can you check the neighbouring stores and properties across the road? Someone else must have CCTV footage covering that part of the street."

"I'm on it," Abby replied, grabbing her bag and disappearing from the cramped small office.

"Mike, let's have a drive around the local streets. Perhaps her car is still close by?" It seemed pointless in Scott's mind, but he needed to do something with the frustration gnawing away at him.

"Where are you, Cara?" Scott whispered, as Mike trawled the streets around the Co-op. His eyes scanned every car in a futile hope that she had left hers parked nearby and had gone off to do something else. *Who am I kidding*? he surmised. His gut instinct told him that Cara had come to harm. He only hoped he wasn't too late.

"There's nothing on this side, guv. Where next?"

"Let's try across the road, Mike. But first, let's track down Abby." Scott reached for his phone.

A few minutes later, Abby jumped into the back of the car and updated the others. "I only found two other places that had CCTV cameras capturing the pavement close to the shops. One was a dead end. The other picked up Cara crossing the road away from the camera before turning left into the next side turning." Abby pointed the way and Mike moved off again, following her instructions. The road was double-parked and difficult to manoeuvre along. An Amazon Prime van crept along the road looking for the correct address.

"Come on, you useless tosser," Mike fumed, flicking on the sirens and gesticulating at the driver to move on. The driver seemed to be in no hurry and crept past, flashing a stare of annoyance at Mike. Mike was about to wind the window down and tear a strip off the man when Scott placed a hand on his arm. Heeding Scott's silent warning, Mike pushed on.

"There! Stop!" Scott shouted.

Mike slammed on the brakes, forcing everyone to fly forward in their seats. Scott jumped out of the car before Mike applied the handbrake.

After racing around Cara's parked car, Scott peered in through the windows, cupping his hands around his eyes, looking for any sign of her or her belongings. He stepped back onto the pavement and glanced up and down the street, looking for any signs of her or anything belonging to her on the ground. Nothing.

.

"We'll start knocking on a few doors to see if anyone's heard or seen anything," Abby said, nudging Mike in the ribs.

The woman he loved had disappeared, and Scott felt powerless. An anxious few minutes passed as he paced up and down the road, trying her phone every few seconds. Each attempt went to voicemail. And each time he heard her voice on the familiar recording, frustration snaked up his spine. Feedback from Abby and Mike did little to calm his nerves. Feeling completely and utterly defeated, Scott stuffed his hands in his pockets and felt a sudden rush of loneliness and vulnerability.

Panic tore through him. The veins in his neck throbbed and his eyes bulged. His mind swirled as his thoughts collided in one cataclysmic storm, drowning out the sounds of passing cars and the conversations around him. Pressure grew inside his head, forcing Scott to lean over a car bonnet and take a large lungful of air. His stomach turned over.

Get a grip! Breathe slowly.

He couldn't prove it, nor did he have the evidence, but deep down he knew Cara had come to harm.

27

M ike and Abby were unsure what to say as Scott
simply stared at his phone. When the silence
became oppressive, Mike broke the stalemate.
"There are a few doors where no one answered. More
than likely students, so they could be back any time. I'll
arrange for a couple of officers to continue the door-to-door
enquiries."

"Thanks, Mike," Scott murmured. "I really appreciate
what you guys are doing. Cara could be anywhere."

Abby leaned forward and popped her head between the
two front seats. "She's not been missing that long. We've got
a really good chance of locating her. I should be getting the
cell site data within the hour. The boss has pushed it
through as a code-red priority with the phone provider."

"I shouldn't have let her go. She was so insistent though.
Bloody stubborn when she wants to be. Thinking about it
now, the voice in that message said that he was going to
screw me up beyond all recognition and take away my

happiness. I know he aimed it at me, but now I see *exactly* what he meant."

Abby placed a hand on his shoulder and listened whilst Mike called through to the office, giving the team an update and putting in a request for extra resources.

"Where to now?" Mike asked after hanging up.

Scott shook his head. "I don't know. Home, I guess. She's been lifted, I just know it. There's no way Cara wouldn't call in or not answer her phone with everything that's going on."

Mike started the car and was buckling up when Scott's phone beeped. Scott scrambled to unlock the screen. It was the arrival of a text message. He didn't recognise the number and it didn't come up on caller ID. The message contained a URL link. He clicked on it and took a gasp of breath.

The sound of Cara screaming filled the inside of the car. Mike and Abby leaned in as Scott began to shake. The video showed Cara tied to a chair in a large, clear tank. Her screams were slightly muffled and terror had widened her eyes.

Scott's hands trembled; he lost grip of the phone and it tumbled into the footwell. He quickly retrieved it as nausea bubbled up. With each second that passed the tingling in his chest grew stronger, and his stomach clenched harder. His vision blurred as the light-headedness kicked in.

Mike could see Scott struggling. He grabbed the phone from him and tossed it to Abby. "Take long deep breaths, guv. Nice and slow."

"I... I... can't... breathe..."

Mike swivelled in his seat. "Look at me, guv. Follow my breathing." Mike drew in long, slow breaths and exhaled even slower. He repeated that a dozen times until Scott had brought his breathing back in line with his own. "That's good. Nice and slow, guv."

Sweat beaded on Scott's forehead. He jammed his hands into his armpits and bent forward. His loud, deep breaths filled the interior. "Please God, no."

Oh my God, Abby mouthed silently, as she stared at the clip in horror. Her eyes moistened and she blinked rapidly, pushing the tears out. She slapped a hand over her mouth to silence the whimpering that threatened to escape from her lips.

At first she hadn't noticed it, but the realisation soon hit her.

This wasn't a video clip. It was a live stream.

28

Scott raced into the station and took the stairs two at a time, headed for Meadows's office. In the meantime, Abby and Mike went back to the team to update them. Abby wanted to do it without Scott around to save him the pain of hearing about Cara's situation again and her pleas for help over the live feed.

"Scott, what are you doing here?" Meadows bellowed from behind his desk. "You are under strict instructions to stay at home!"

Scott wasn't in any mood to have a slanging match with Meadows. He shut the door to the office and collapsed into a seat opposite his boss. His body felt weary, and his mind felt frayed, as if he were hanging on the edge of a precipice and his fingers were slowly losing grip.

"Cara's been abducted," Scott said, resting his elbows on his knees and burying his face in his hands.

"What?" Meadows said, unsure he'd heard correctly.

"She's been kidnapped. I received a text message with a link to a live video feed. Cara's being held against her will."

Meadows furrowed his brow. "Was she not with you... at home?"

Scott nodded. "Yes. But then she insisted on popping out to the shops and also wanted to pick up work from the office, so she could spend more time at home with me." He continued to explain the circumstances, the words tumbling from his mouth in a jumbled mess.

"And you've scoured the area where she was last seen?"

"Yes," Scott hissed. "Where she was last seen and where her vehicle was found. Mike pulled a few members of the team to that location to continue door-to-door enquiries." Scott dragged his hand down his face. "I don't know if that will help. Something is better than nothing."

"Where is your phone now?"

"Abby's got it. Matt's team is going to look at the feed. See if they can pull any location or source data off it."

Meadows stood up from his chair and came around to Scott. "I will liaise with Matt and his team. In the meantime, get someone to take you home. We'll handle it."

Scott jumped from his chair and squared up to Meadows. Just inches apart, he stared at his boss. "I'm not going anywhere. He's taken Cara, and she's carrying our baby. If you expect me to sit on my arse and wait patiently, then forget it."

Meadows stiffened, annoyed at being challenged. "I know what you're saying, Scott, but we need the team working on this. They are focused and thinking clearly. In your current state, you're not doing either. You'll make the situation worse."

Scott slapped a hand on the desk. "With all due respect, this is my girlfriend and our baby we're talking about. My number one priority is getting them back safely. I think that's focused... don't you?"

"I appreciate what you're saying, Scott. This is personal. Whoever has taken Cara wants to provoke a reaction in you. He wants to get you out in the open, so you're exposed. If you charge around trying to find him, you're playing straight into his hands. At least if you're at home, our officers can protect you."

Scott's lids twitched with anger. "It's not me that needs protecting. It's him. He's picked the wrong person to mess with and placing my family in danger means I have no choice but to track him down myself."

Meadows fell silent for a few minutes as he studied Scott. Then he nodded once. "I could officially order you to stay at home and if you broke the instruction, you'd be subject to a disciplinary procedure. In these circumstances, that would only add more angst to what you're already feeling." Meadows stepped back to put space between them. "I'm prepared to let you re-join the team but Abby is still the acting SIO, understand?"

Scott reluctantly agreed.

"The high-tech unit has remotely installed tracking software on your job phone. It will monitor and trace every phone call you receive and every call you make. We do this by the book and follow due process, understand?"

"Yep, crystal clear." Scott didn't hang around for any more of Meadows's pep talk. He marched out of the office.

29

The team fell silent when Scott walked in. His steps slowed. He glanced around at the officers. Keyboards and phones fell silent. Officers in small huddles paused their conversations and turned in his direction. Others swivelled in their chairs with concern and compassion in their eyes as they looked on.

"You okay, guv?" Raj asked, and then tutted at his own stupidity. "Sorry, guv. You know what I mean. Stupid question."

Scott patted him on the shoulder and returned a weak smile before nodding. "Yep, stupid question."

He headed to the front of the room where Abby was gathering her notes after the quick update she'd given to the team on the latest developments, including Cara's abduction and the live video feed sent to Scott's phone.

"I've told everyone. They're pretty cut up," Abby offered.

Scott knew as much. He sensed the awkwardness, with many not knowing what to say. Clearing his throat, he turned to face the sea of concerned expressions.

"Thank you all for your hard work. This isn't easy for me," he said, sighing. "Someone clearly has it in for me. I don't know who and I don't know why, but I'm relying on all of you to help Abby as acting SIO to track down the person responsible." His eyes travelled around the group. "With Cara missing the stakes are high. Please find her."

Abby felt the pain in Scott's heartfelt plea that tinged his last few words. His anguish saddened her beyond words.

Scott spent the next hour grabbing snippets of information from various members of the team. The investigation into the graveyard desecration had left more questions than answers. Forensics couldn't recover any evidence, and door-to-door enquiries had yielded nothing of importance. The efforts the team were making in tracking down all known suspects and criminals attached to the cases on which Scott had been SIO encouraged him.

Despite his best efforts to stay positive, the lack of progress and solid leads only dampened his mood further. Mike had reached out to several of his informants and, though he was waiting on one or two to get back to him, the rest hadn't been able to help either.

Scott slumped down in a chair next to Abby's desk as his chest heaved. He drew in a long, deep breath and released it. "This isn't getting us anywhere," he murmured to no one in particular.

Abby turned in her chair and leaned in, keeping her voice down. "We have to stay positive. Look around you. The team is working their nuts off. We couldn't ask any more of them."

Scott grimaced as he looked around the office. There wasn't a single officer sitting around doing nothing. Everyone was either tapping away on their computers or in deep discussion on the phone. A few desks were vacant where officers were out following up on enquiries.

It seemed an eternity before his personal phone rang. Scott grabbed it from inside his jacket pocket and stared at the screen, scared to touch any of the buttons. He didn't recognise the number, but looked at Abby, who nodded. Silence filled the room as every officer stopped what they were doing and looked in his direction. The hairs bristled on the back of his neck and his palms felt sweaty.

Scott let it ring off. A few seconds later his job phone rang.

Scott lifted that phone from the desk and finally pressed the green button. "Hello."

The caller's voice was muffled and quiet. "I took you by surprise, didn't I? Your girlfriend was being sloppy. I think we should play a game if you want to see Cara again."

Scott's eyelids flickered as a flash of searing anger shot through him. Mention of Cara's name made him clench his free hand into a tight fist. *Who is he to call her by her first name? As if he knows her personally?*

"What do you want?"

"No need to rush. I've got plenty of time. Though Cara hasn't. If you waste my time, I'll just leave her and let the tank fill up. I can imagine how you'd feel to see Cara drowning..."

Scott rose and pressed the phone tighter to his ear. "If you hurt her, I'll hunt you down for the rest of my living days. I'll make sure you get put away for the rest of your miserable life."

The man fell silent for a few moments.

Scott gritted his teeth as guilt flooded his body. *Did I jeopardise the situation even further? Did I blow my chance?*

"Are you still there?" he asked.

"I'm still here. Your threats don't bother me. I've lost everything. That's your fault. My only goal in life now is to make you pay. Now... back to what I was saying. I think it's time we played a game. Pavilion Gardens. You will find a mobile phone in one of the bins. You'll get further instructions then. The cleaners will empty the bins within an hour."

The line went dead.

30

Officers swarmed from the station and jumped into all available vehicles before screeching from the station car park. Pedestrians looked on in surprise as a convoy of police cars raced the short distance on blue lights and wailing sirens. Pavilion Gardens was a few minutes from the station, though the brief journey felt like an eternity to Scott. He shifted in his seat whilst Abby steered her vehicle through the traffic.

"I swear I'm going to –"

Abby interrupted Scott. "We need to stay cool and focused. We don't know who we're dealing with, and we don't know how volatile he might be. Every time he contacts us, that's a bit more evidence for us."

"Yes, I know, Abby," Scott replied. "We don't even know his actual voice because he disguises it every time. This isn't something that's just happening. He's been planning this for over a year." Scott paused for a moment. "Sorry, I didn't mean to snap."

"We'll get her back," Abby said, tapping his thigh as she pulled into a side turning. Because of its location, it wasn't an easy place to get access to by vehicle, and the closest she could get to it was the Pavilion Buildings off North Street. Other police vehicles pulled in behind her, with the rest stopping on North Street.

Shoppers and diners looked on in confusion as Scott ran from the vehicle and through an imposing archway which led to the Royal Pavilion on his right-hand side. Abby joined him along with the other officers, and soon over twenty of them had assembled.

Scott glanced around. *For fuck's sake, it could be anywhere.*

Paths led off in different directions, many of them lined with well-established trees. Ornate, thigh-high, green railings skirted the boundaries of the path. A chilling thought crossed his mind. Perhaps Cara's abductor was watching them right now. But there were too many people here for Scott to pick out any one individual. Tourists ambled along, cameras slung around their necks, taking in the serene gardens set against the magnificent domes of the Pavilion. Locals and students scurried along the pathways using the gardens as a shortcut.

Abby didn't wait for Scott to say anything. As acting SIO, she needed to command the troops. "We need to split up and check every single bin within the grounds. Check and double-check them. It's a shit job. Be careful when you are examining the contents. Other than the usual rubbish, there could be needles, so glove up and approach with caution." She snapped on her own latex gloves. The gardens were a notorious spot for the homeless to congregate, many of whom were drunk or incapacitated through drugs.

The officers headed off in different directions, whilst Scott went with Abby and searched a different area of the gardens.

Scott's temples throbbed and he clenched his fists. He needed to do this by the book but felt an overwhelming urge to corner and beat the crap out of Cara's abductor. The stakes had never been higher. Not only was Cara at risk, but their baby had been put in harm's way. That was unforgivable in Scott's mind.

Abby nervously glanced at the time on her phone. She had already given instructions to all the officers to keep an eye out for the council workers and to stop them from emptying any of the waste bins until they had completed the search.

They stopped beside a small, green metal bin sat beneath a mature tree. Searching the bin would play right into Abby's OCD, but she wasn't about to let Scott down. She pulled the door open and retrieved the silver bin from within. Abby scrunched her nose and shuddered as she peered inside.

This is so gross.

Reaching in, she swirled her hand around, disturbing its contents, and stirring up the vile smell coming from half-eaten sandwiches, apple cores, and banana skins. Mixed amongst them were sandwich containers, drinks cans, used tissues, and discarded magazines.

"Anything?" Scott asked, as he searched for the next closest bin.

"Nope, nothing. Bollocks."

"Let's move on." Scott was already marching off to the next one before Abby had removed her dirty hand from the bin. Closing her eyes and almost retching in the process, she ripped off her gloves and tossed them into the bin before snapping on a fresh pair.

The lack of feedback from other officers heightened Scott's anxiety. Thirty minutes of searching hadn't uncovered the mobile phone. Scott wondered if they'd been sent on a wild goose chase. He continued to scan the crowd, casting his eye farther to the boundary of the gardens, in case someone was lurking on a neighbouring street, watching them from a distance.

"This is getting us nowhere. He's winding us up!" Scott growled through gritted teeth.

Scott and Abby jogged around the perimeter close to Brighton Dome. Having searched the ground, they were fast running out of options. The route took them to the pedestrian area opposite the Theatre Royal, a popular spot for eateries, which only saddened Scott further. He'd only just been here, walking the streets with Cara, after they'd celebrated their one-year anniversary.

Mike caught up with them. "We've found nothing, guv. We've searched the bins twice."

Scott shook his head in frustration, hanging onto his sanity by his fingertips.

Abby rested her hands on her hips as she looked around. "Look, there's a bin fixed to the wall of the dome. It's still in the gardens, but not as visible." She raced towards it before she'd finished her sentence. Mike and Scott were hot on her heels.

She couldn't access the contents and had to root around blindly. Her fingers touched a solid object and she wrapped her hand around it. A phone!

She pulled it out handed it to Scott, who scanned the screen. He opened the messaging app and found one short sentence.

Your next clue is where seven roads meet.

31

Scott groaned and shook his head in confusion whilst looking around. It felt like the buildings were closing in on him, squashing him between the grips of a vice.

"What the hell is he playing at?" he growled, as he handed the phone to Abby and headed back in towards the gardens with Mike in tow.

Abby scanned the message, following a few steps behind.

She caught up with him on one pathway, just as other officers made their way towards him. Abby instructed several of the officers to head back to the location of the bin and search for any CCTV in the vicinity. She hoped that many of the eateries would have cameras. The question in her mind was whether any of them looked out across the pedestrian precinct or gardens and the location of the bin. Abby hoped that Cara's abductor may have been seen depositing the phone in the bin.

With most officers now gathered around Scott and aware of the clue, it soon became clear that it referred to the Seven

Dials, a location five minutes' drive east from their current position, where seven roads intersected.

They were back in their cars moments later racing along Dyke Road. Scott didn't have time to think. He scanned the buildings they passed, a mixture of Regency style properties, characterised by their pale stuccoed exteriors with classic-style mouldings and bay windows to his right. To his left, recent stylish apartments with smoked windows and brilliant-white brickwork catered for the trendy urbanites who wanted calmer surroundings but were close enough to the buzz of the city centre.

Scott pulled out his phone. Though every bone in his body dreaded the thought of what he would see, he needed to check on Cara. He needed to feel connected with her.

His body stiffened as he clicked on the live feed. The muscles in his jaws flexed. Cara shivered. Panic and confusion twisted her features, as if she'd been crying a thousand tears. Every sinew of his being wanted to jump through the screen of his phone and be there to rescue Cara. Guilt poisoned his thoughts. It was his fault she was in this position.

Abby swung a left at the Seven Dials roundabout and pulled up on a pavement. Three other pool cars stopped behind her. The officers gathered with Mike, Abby, and Scott at the front. They stood for a few moments taking in their surroundings, unsure what to do next. The first message had given them clear instructions; however, the vagueness of the second did little to help them.

"What are we supposed to do now?" Mike asked, raising his arms. "Seven roads. Lots of shops. Has he left a note? Another phone? Is it one of the shops?"

Scott turned in a full circle on the spot. Three of the

roads ended with retail outlets. A bakery, a pub, and a dry cleaner. Various other shops snaked along the side roads from those points. Residential properties finished the remaining roads that led to the roundabout.

Officers spread out with a few visiting the shops to find out if any customers had been acting suspiciously or had left something behind. Others searched the area for waste bins.

Abby shook her head. "He's been very clever, guv. I can only see one set of cameras," she said, jabbing a finger at the bakery and its seating area on the pavement. She saw one of her officers darting into the doorway of the bakery. "We'll know in a few moments whether the cameras have a wide-angle view of the area."

Scott took a deep breath and closed his eyes for a few moments. Though he was trying to stay objective, his heart ached. Every minute that passed felt like an hour. He needed to save her.

He opened open his eyes and looked over his shoulder at a roundabout. Something in his subconscious told him to stand in the middle. He turned and darted through the traffic before coming to a stop. Alone, he let his eyes drift over his surroundings. *What am I supposed to find?*

Mike joined him a few moments later. "Guv?"

"I don't know, Mike. His clue must be in plain sight."

"We've searched all the usual spots. The bins are empty. The shopkeepers haven't noticed anything suspicious."

Scott stared at the ground. The roundabout was made of blockwork and cobbled stones, level and flat with the surrounding roads. Oblong in shape, they had a large metal grommet positioned on each corner. Two trees were on the island, surrounded by a small grass apron.

Scott's thoughts raced as he tracked back through all the

conversations over the last hour. "When he called last time, he referred to the Pavilion Gardens and then the wastepaper bins."

Mike nodded in agreement.

"The text message only referred to where seven roads met. He didn't refer to the shops or surrounding streets. He made a direct reference to this." Scott pointed to the ground. His eyes travelled up into the trees. Cogs in his mind worked furiously, connecting the dots. He hurried towards one tree, whilst pointing for Mike to head to the other. Scott looked up towards its branches, looking for any signs of a package or a bag. Nothing.

He knelt down and rummaged through the tall grass. His eyes widened when the tips of his fingers touched a solid object. He pushed the blades of grass apart. Another mobile phone.

"Mike!" Scott shouted.

Mike hurried over and leaned over his shoulder. Scott pressed the power button. Again, this phone wasn't locked. One text message. Scott took a deep breath as he opened it. Another clue.

Rest in peace with St Nicholas.

32

"St Nicholas?!" Scott stared at the message before looking around at his assembled officers.

"Guv, St Nicholas, aka the Wonderworker, and Santa Claus. Known as the miracle worker too," an officer said.

Scott gritted his teeth the more he thought about it. The sarcasm Cara's abductor was displaying only infuriated him further. He was taunting Scott. Only a miracle from St Nicholas could save Cara.

"Rest in peace..." Abby mumbled whilst searching Google on her phone. "All the locations so far have been within five minutes of each other. Station to Pavilion. Pavilion to Seven Dials. There's a St Nicholas Church less than five minutes from here.... Coincidence?" Abby asked, turning to Scott.

Scott shrugged. The vagueness of the clues could be interpreted in many ways, but with little to go on, Scott bought into Abby's line of thinking. "Mike, can you head back to the office and liaise with Matt? He's getting the voice recordings analysed. We need to analyse this video feed and the phones as a priority. Anything around IP links, locations and those kinds of things?"

Mike nodded and shot off towards his car.

A few minutes later, Abby pulled up outside St Nicholas Church and exited the car alongside Scott. He crossed his arms and let out a deep sigh. The poignancy of the location wasn't lost on him.

"It's another graveyard," Scott said. It was late afternoon and the sun was dipping down behind the clouds. The eerie shadows cast by tombstones across the overgrown grass added to the gloomy surrounds. "Where are we supposed to look?"

"It's too big an area for us and a handful of officers. I'm going to draft in extra resources. In the meantime, we can at least start our search." Abby instructed officers to form a line along one boundary wall, keeping the space between them to only a few feet. They shuffled along, scanning the ground and treading through the long grass. It felt like a fruitless exercise in her mind, but until extra resources arrived, they had to push on.

The frustration was palpable amongst the officers. Several of them kicked the grass with their feet as they wove their way through the gravestones. With darkness not far away, many of the officers had resorted to using torches they had retrieved from the cars to help them in their search.

Thirty minutes later, two personnel carriers and a dog unit arrived. As news spread amongst CID, some off-duty officers turned up to help, knowing how much this meant to all of them. Abby deployed them in the search, allowing them to cover a much greater area. The search continued with pace as darkness crept in. Abby saw the panic in Scott's eyes as he teetered on the edge. His voice fluctuated in pitch and volume every time he spoke, and he kept clenching and unclenching his fists. Time wasn't on their side, and she knew it. They all knew it.

"Please tell me someone has got something?" Abby shouted to no one in particular. The lack of responses told her all she needed to know.

She watched as the sniffer dog darted left and right, nose down, tail up, with its handler encouraging it on. It worked ahead of them so that they didn't lay down false trails of human scent that would interfere with the search.

The search team had covered half of the grounds when Scott stopped in his tracks. He looked over the small stone and flint wall of the church grounds at a sign tucked into an archway across the road.

"Bollocks! We've been looking in the wrong place. The gardens of rest are across the road. That's what he meant when he said, 'Rest in peace!'" Scott shouted, jabbing his finger.

Abby followed his line of sight. Across the road was another cemetery hidden behind a tall hedgerow which skirted its boundary. A stone archway with a wrought-iron gate signalled the entrance to St Nicholas's Garden of Rest.

33

Searchlights arced left and right as officers searched the new location late into the evening. Many of them were cold and hungry but determined to not give up. The police sniffer dog had failed to pick up a trace which only exacerbated the tension further. Lines of officers snaked across the grass searching for anything, but in the dark, they knew finding another mobile phone would be a miracle.

Scott had joined several officers in one line, whilst Abby had teamed up with another group searching a different part of the grounds. The scale of the task wasn't lost on any of them. The grounds were bigger than those surrounding the church, with paths, more mature trees, and a burgeoning hedge that hemmed the gardens in.

Scott checked his phone and the live feed of Cara every few minutes. Sometimes Cara would be awake, scanning her surroundings, and other times her head bowed, as if asleep. He spoke into his phone hoping his voice would reach her, but disappointment sat with him when she never responded. Dipping out of his line, he leaned against a tree and slid to the ground. He tucked his knees into his chest and buried his face in his hands. The sense of isolation and helplessness ate away at him.

Abby joined him a few moments later and knelt beside him. "Stupid question I know, but how are you holding up?"

He shook his head. "It's like I'm in the worst nightmare ever. I can't get my head around this. I can't see how we can get to Cara. We've got no leads and a maniac is sending us on this twisted treasure hunt around Brighton. Cara could be held anywhere in Brighton, Sussex... or even farther." Tears filled Scott's eyes. He swallowed hard as he fought to focus.

Abby wrapped her arms around Scott. He welcomed her warmth, and he buried his head into her shoulder and sobbed. He clung onto her like he was hanging onto life itself, scared to let go.

"Scott, you can't give up. Cara needs you. Your baby needs you. Meadows has drafted in extra officers from outside of Brighton to help in the search. We are throwing every available resource into finding her. Matt's relying on every technological tool he has at his disposal. The vessel Cara's being held in is our most promising clue. We might get a lead off it, since it's not the type of thing you could pop down to B&Q and buy. It's something more specialised. I've asked the team to do a national search for manufacturers. I mean, how many can there be? That list may help us to identify any recent purchases." She stroked the back of his head, trying to comfort him. "We're going to do this together. We're going to find Cara."

Scott nodded and sniffed loudly. "Thank you," he whispered.

Abby stood up and held out her hands. She pulled Scott back up to his feet. "You ready to carry on searching?"

Scott sighed and nodded.

They headed back through the trees towards a moving wall of light that broke through the darkness, and joined the nearest search team. Abby got an update from the PolSA coordinator leading that group of officers who reported nothing of significance other than the discovery of a discarded knife that appeared to have been there for a while.

As they continued to search, the line of officers paused when they heard a phone ringing. They looked at each other before directing their searchlights near where the noise was coming from. Scott and the others hurried towards the source, scanning the ground. The ringing stopped. The frustration grew.

"Bollocks!" Scott shouted. "Did anyone pick up a rough location?"

A mixture of replies came, but many of the officers agreed that the ringing had come from somewhere over towards the right. As a group they moved in that direction, their torches swaying from left to right across the grass.

A few minutes passed before the phone rang again. This time louder. The officer closest to it homed in on its precise location.

"It's here!" he shouted, directing his torch at a phone on the ground.

Scott raced over to it and snapped on a pair of latex gloves before reaching down to pick it up. He didn't recognise the number. He glanced at Abby who stood rooted to the spot.

"Hello?" Scott answered. All he heard was a man's laughter on the other end. Hysterical laughter. "Who is this?"

The laughter subsided.

"You took your time finding it. If only you had been more thorough, you wouldn't have wasted so much time across the road."

"What do you want?" Scott hissed. "Give me a time and place to meet you, and I'll come alone. Just let Cara go first."

The man sighed. "No, that would be too easy. I need you to suffer."

"Don't you think I'm suffering enough already?" Scott's tone was acidic.

"No," came the reply. "By the way, I thought that was quite a touching moment earlier between you and Abby. It's nice that you have a shoulder to cry on."

Scott's eyes widened as he searched the surrounding gloom. With the phone on loudspeaker, the officers around Scott heard every word, and looked around, shining their torches.

The man laughed again. "Tell the others to stop looking. It won't do any good. You won't find me. I'll be in touch."

"Wait!" Scott shouted before the line went dead. "Fucker!" Scott screamed. "He's watching us right now. He's been watching us all this time. Everyone, search for a camera. There must be a camera with night vision capability fixed to a post, a tree trunk, a bench, anything that would offer a mounting point."

The officers fanned out in different directions, their searchlights scanning up and down trees, picking out garden benches, and hunting down more wastepaper bins. A few minutes passed and extra officers flooded in to join the search. A shout in the darkness had all officers converging to the spot where a female officer stood at the base of a tree. She was pointing the light from her torch up to the nearest branch.

Scott arrived seconds later and stared up at the branch where a small, camouflaged IR camera often used by wildlife enthusiasts had been secured. The small, red sensor glowed in the darkness.

The phone rang again from the same number.

"Congratulations. Smile for the camera."

The line went dead.

34

He hadn't been back to the barn since capturing Cara. He'd considered not returning here at all, since he wasn't interested in her. After all, she was collateral damage.

After unlocking the padlock, he stepped into the darkened space. It was time to check that she was still alive. The woman being dead wouldn't help him at all. Not so early in the game, anyway. He wanted Scott to suffer. Really suffer. He wanted to break the man. It pleased him to see Scott race around the city on a wild goose chase looking for cameras and phones. They were easy to buy online, and he had covered his tracks well by using a credit card under a stolen identity.

The barn had no heating, lighting, or electricity, so he'd planned ahead. A small array of battery banks had been wired up to power the laptop. He'd brought a fresh supply with him and swapped them out. The camera still pointed in the right direction, but the darkness hampered the clarity of the image on the live feed.

He'd considered bringing food and water for Cara but decided he didn't give a shit whether she went hungry or got dehydrated. As he looked at the Perspex tank, the thought of having to scale it and get in with her didn't appeal to him in the slightest. When he had first set the tank in place, he'd brought a collapsible ladder with him, but having no use for it, he'd taken it back home. With Cara in there, he had no intention of taking her out.

Satisfied that his computer would stay on, he moved over to the Perspex and leaned against it, tapping the torchlight feature on his phone. It cast a bright light which lit up his surroundings. Holding it against the Perspex, the light diffused and offered a faint glow which illuminated Cara.

As his eyes scanned her limp body, he felt nothing for her. Her hands were secured to the chair; her head remained bowed and didn't move when the light touched her face.

"Oi. Wake up." He hammered on the tank with a fist when a thought flashed in his mind. Was she dead already? He banged his fist harder. "I said... wake up."

Cara flinched in the chair. She slowly raised her head, her matted hair stuck to her face. The colour had drained from her skin. She looked pale and clammy. Her eyes looked lifeless as she blinked hard, adjusting to the harsh light.

"Good. For a minute I thought you were dead. Not that it matters to me, but I want you to hang around for a bit longer. I'm not finished with you. You're wondering why Scott hasn't rescued you yet?" Crossing his arms, he continued to shine the light towards her. "I don't think he's bothered, to be honest. I don't think you mean that much to him. You see he's still grieving over the loss of his family. You are just a nice, little stopgap to take away the pain."

Cara opened her mouth, her lips dry, cracked and bleeding. "Please..." she whispered. "Please help me. Please let me go..." She lowered her head again.

He shook his head. "Your time will come soon. Scott will have another two graves to visit before I'm done with him. He'll have a choice to make. The real question is whether he'll save you." He switched off the light on his phone and turned, not feeling anything for the woman he had abducted.

35

Scott and the team arrived back at the office in the early hours. Like Scott, the others collapsed in chairs, exhausted and hungry. Several support officers manning the phones dashed off to the kitchen to make coffee and sandwiches.

Scott felt numb having spent most of the journey staring at his phone and the live feed of Cara. She had gone through moments of wakefulness before tiredness crept up on her.

"Here's a coffee for you, guv," a support officer said, placing a mug beside him. "Is there anything else I can get you? We're rustling up sandwiches and ordering a few pizzas. Can I make you something?"

"Thanks, but I'm not hungry. I appreciate the offer though." Scott sighed.

"Guv, you've got to eat something," Abby said, pulling up a chair alongside him. She suggested that the support officer should whip up a sandwich.

"What am I going to do, Abby? I feel so bloody helpless.

He took her this morning, and it's now one a.m. and we still haven't found her."

"We are doing everything we can. We've checked the source of the envelopes. The door-to-door enquiries around the cemetery in Bear Road are done and in the next few hours we should have the voice analysis."

Scott shook his head. "It's not enough."

"I know. We've seized the infrared camera. Officers found another one in the grounds of the church. He's been watching us the whole time. They're being examined for prints and their transmission protocols. What we don't know is the transmission range of those devices. It will help us find out if he was close by."

"He's even more twisted than I thought if he was that close." Scott looked up from sipping his coffee to see Mike and Matt coming through the main doors and making their way towards him.

Matt pulled up a chair and sat in silence with Scott for a few moments. He rubbed his bloodshot eyes and pulled his shoulders back, to ease the ache. "I've looked at the live video feed but haven't found the IP link. I think the feed is being cloaked. It makes it hard to find the source."

Scott furrowed his brow and massaged his aching temples. On a clear day he struggled to understand Matt's terminology, but in his state of exhaustion, the words went in one ear and out of the other. "Break it down for me, mate. Plain language, please."

Matt nodded. "Sorry, mate. I'll try my best. We all know that whenever someone uses the internet, they're assigned an IP address. An internet protocol address. A series of digits and dots. This magic number holds important details and when you visit a website, it lays down a digital breadcrumb trail that includes location and who your internet provider is."

Scott nodded as he tried to keep up. Abby pulled in her chair closer.

"The IP address gives us an idea of someone's where-abouts, but a user can hide their location using a proxy." Matt paused, feeling the need to elaborate. "A proxy server is a system or router that provides a gateway between users and the internet. There are lots of proxies out there," he added, waving his hand, "but when a link is sent through a proxy, it redirects the traffic through a proxy server. It's the proxy server IP that we see and not the real IP."

"And our man is using that?" Abby asked.

Matt shook his head. "No, he's too clever for that. Most use free proxies that have trackers, so you're giving up too much information to the proxy server."

"What is he using?" Abby probed.

"We reckon he's using a VPN, a virtual private network or a Tor. It changes your location and encrypts your traffic. It creates a protective shield when you are using unsecured networks like public Wi-Fi hotspots."

"And... this Tor thing? What's that?" Scott fired back.

"The Tor stands for The Onion Router. This is a further level of protection, wrapping online traffic in several layers of encryption to keep it safe from prying eyes. You can think of this encryption like the layers of an onion." Matt checked Scott was still with him before he continued. "Again, free, it protects a user's anonymity by bouncing their communica-tions through a distribution network of relays run by volun-teers around the world. It prevents us from seeing what sites they visit, as well as determining their physical location. It means that the final feed we're getting could bounce to us from a router in Brazil, New Zealand, Russia, India – pretty much anywhere on the global map."

Scott squeezed his eyes tight.

Abby looked at Matt, who shrugged his shoulders as if to suggest, "We're fucked."

Matt needed to continue even though he knew how much it hurt Scott to hear his feedback. "It's not impossible for us to trace the general internet usage across URLs around the planet, but it makes it impossible when the perpetrator is using Tor or something similar."

Scott stared up at the ceiling. "You're saying we've got no way of tracking him or finding Cara's location?"

"It's not impossible. I'm reaching out to a colleague who knows someone, who knows someone else in the Intelligence Services. Old university contacts. Anyway, this individual spends all his time tracking internet communications and doing digital forensic analysis on embedded data feeds." Matt stood up and stuffed his hands in his pockets, just as Meadows came through the double doors. "It's a long shot, but I'm hoping they can shed light on our situation. All we need is a rough location of where the camera or laptop might be."

36

Scott sat in Abby's car, deep in reflection. His emotions were bouncing around like a rollercoaster ride, slowing sometimes to a point where he felt nothing, before he rode another wave of intense feelings that threatened to overwhelm him.

Not long after Meadows had come into his office, he had demanded that Scott go home to rest and leave it to the night shift to keep working the case. He'd been so adamant, he'd guided Scott through the building and to the back door. Scott had wanted to push back and fight to stay, but Meadows hadn't been having any of it. He had asked Abby to drive Scott home.

Scott had agreed and thought that a shower and change of clothes would help him stay awake.

"Are you okay?" Abby asked, coming to a stop outside Scott's house. Following a change of shift, armed officers remained in place in an unmarked black BMW 3 series parked across the road.

Scott stared out at the darkness then shrugged.

"Come on, let's get you inside. I'll put the kettle on whilst you grab a shower."

Scott shook his head. "No, it's fine. You head home. You need to rest. Besides, I've just got this anxiety ball in the pit of my stomach. Our man has gone radio silent since the last call. Cara's been trapped in a goldfish bowl for a day now. I don't know if I'll ever see her again..." Scott trailed off, as he opened the car door and stepped out into the cool night air.

Abby followed him up the garden path. "Scott, don't talk like that. We'll find her. I promise." She wanted to sound genuine, and deep down she was desperate to find Cara for Scott's sake. But her mind kept running through worst-case scenarios.

Scott flicked on the hall light and headed through to the kitchen where he reached for a glass and an opened bottle of Jack Daniel's. He poured himself a hefty measure and brought the glass up to his lips.

Abby placed a hand on his arm. "No, Scott. We need you sober. I won't let you drink yourself into a shit state."

Scott's lips trembled and he headed for the lounge, leaving Abby standing in the kitchen. He flipped on the light switch and dropped onto the sofa before burying his head in his hands. Abby followed and took a seat beside him. She placed a hand on his knee, rubbing it for reassurance.

His shoulders shook as he cried into his hands. Abby pulled him into an embrace. As if that small act of kindness gave him permission to let go, sobs wracked his body and anguished cries tore from his throat. Seeing the man she cared for cry like a little boy only added to her upset. Tears filled her eyes as she chewed on her bottom lip.

"Sssh. We'll get through this. You're not alone," she offered, as Scott cried into her shoulder. There was so much she wanted to say to reassure him but doubted anything would make a difference. He had held it together in front of everyone at the station but had reached a breaking point. His mental faculties were in meltdown through a combination of stress, worry, and weariness.

For the time being, Abby was going to hold him as long as he needed.

37

"Shit!" Scott shouted, as he jumped up from the sofa.

Abby jolted awake, blinking furiously as she looked around, confused at her surroundings.

Scott grabbed his phone to check the time. It was seven a.m. They had fallen asleep for six hours.

"Shit," he shouted again, as his phone bleeped and the screen went dead. Scott raced into the kitchen in search of a charger, with Abby not far behind. He pulled open drawers before slamming them shut. His eyes searched every square inch of the kitchen before he darted from the room and raced upstairs to his bedroom.

"Scott, slow down!" Abby shouted, as she ran up the steps after him.

"You don't understand, Abby. He might try to contact me right now. Something might have happened to Cara and I wouldn't know." He yanked open a bedside drawer and found a spare charger. Jamming the plug into a socket and the other end into his phone, he pleaded for it to activate.

The empty battery icon appeared and flashed as the phone charged.

"Come on! Come on!" Scott hissed, as he pressed the power button and waited for the screen to turn on.

Abby waited in the doorway. Scott's agitated state worried her, but she knew better than to intervene when he was like this.

Scott's eyes widened when the screen came alive. It took a few moments before all the icons were refreshed. He clicked on his messages and found the link to the live feed. It was too long for Scott before the video feed appeared. Cara's head was bowed, and he wondered if she was alive.

He wanted to cry. He wanted to scream. His chest felt tight, as if an imaginary source had sucked all the air from his lungs.

"Cara!" Scott screamed. "Cara, wake up. It's me. We're going to find you!"

The one-way feed only tortured Scott further. They could hear her, but she couldn't hear them.

"Please... please wake up. I love you. I'm not going to let you go." Scott dropped to his knees beside the bed, the weight of pain too heavy for him to carry. His body felt loose and limp; he had no more energy left.

Abby came around to his side of the bed and crouched down beside him.

"Give me the phone, Scott," she said, holding her hand out for it. He didn't move. "Scott... give me the phone. I will watch it whilst you have a shower. Freshen yourself up, get a change of clothes, and we'll head into the office as soon as you're ready."

"But –"

"There are no buts, Scott. I'll sit here and watch that

screen. If *anything* changes, then I'll give you a shout. The longer you sit around here, the later we are going to get into the office. Now, go," Abby demanded.

Scott handed over the phone to Abby, his eyes pleading with her to hold up her side of the bargain.

She nodded. "I'm here. Hurry. I'll get an update from the team whilst I'm waiting for you."

38

Scott came back into the bedroom ten minutes later, his hair damp. He'd thrown on a pair of jeans and a dark-blue polo jumper. He'd lingered in the shower longer than he'd wanted to, but the hot spray of water jabbing his body had soothed his aching muscles and lifted the tension that had stiffened his neck and shoulders.

"How are you feeling?" Abby asked, still perched on the end of his bed.

"Better. Anything?" he asked, hopping on one foot as he put on a sock.

Abby shook her head. "Nothing has come back so far on the location of the live feed. He made the phone calls from unregistered numbers."

"Burners..."

Abby nodded. "We're contacting local supermarkets and phone retailers to see if anyone purchased a large quantity of pay-as-you-go phones. The IP link is cloaked. I spoke to Raj. Swann has an alibi, so it's not him. They've noticed another name. Nick Newman. He lives in Reigate. We had local officers attend to interview him. He can't account for his movements, and he lives alone."

"Of interest?" Scott asked.

"Possibly. He's not high on our priority list. Officers spoke to neighbours, and he's a bit of a loner. He doesn't have any visitors. We've also taken the precaution of seizing his car and laptop. They're checking his phone and internet records now."

Abby explained his connection with Scott; it was another criminal who carried the usual grudge of being convicted and sent away. Nothing in his records suggesting that he'd lost anyone or anything lowered Newman's importance.

Scott sat on another corner of the bed and stared at the floor. He shook his head. "Who is this bloke?"

"That's what we're trying to find out."

"I don't get it. Why is he doing this? To dig up someone's grave..." Scott swallowed hard. Flashbacks stole his breath away. "The ring. The photos. He's been following me for a year. Maybe more? He's invaded my privacy. To think that I was out with Cara, enjoying my time with her, and all along there was someone not far away, hiding in the shadows, taking pictures. For fuck's sake, he watched Cara walking up my path and coming into my house. The bastard was outside."

Abby noticed Scott's shoulders stiffen as he drew a sharp intake of breath. His hands tightened into clenched fists. "Scott, I don't know what to say. We need to focus on finding him and making sure that we do things by the book. Once he's put away, he can't hurt you."

Scott turned to Abby, a pained expression haunting his features. "That's the problem. He's already hurt me. He knows that. Single-handedly, he has destroyed the one precious place I could go for quiet reflection –Tina's grave. He's spoiled my memories of being with Cara. And now he's taken her away."

Abby placed a hand on his arm. "And we'll get her back. Matt is doing all he can to track down the source of this live feed. He's going through *different* channels to speed this up. If we'd put in an official request, it could have taken days or weeks to secure approval from somewhere within a governmental department." Abby tutted. "Even then, it would have got tied up in red tape and may never have reached the desk of a communications analyst at GCHQ, or wherever these bods sit."

Scott appreciated Abby's reassurance, but dread twisted his innards. He felt an impending doom as if Cara was slipping away from him.

"This is personal. For him and for me. The only problem is I don't know why." Scott stood and retrieved a pair of shoes from his cupboard. He was about to lace them up when his phone bleeped to announce a text message. Abby scrambled to grab the phone from beside her. She handed it straight to Scott.

Nerves tingled her fingers. She didn't take her eyes off Scott as he read the message.

"It's him," he uttered.

39

S cott stood rooted to the spot. Part of him wanted to scream, whilst the other wanted to throw the phone against the wall in disbelief. Abby pushed him to read the message aloud, but her voice melted into the background as his thoughts consumed him. *When will this nightmare end?* His eyes clamped shut, as an image of him standing in front of Cara's coffin hit him with the force of a thunderbolt. *Déjà vu repeating itself.*

"Scott... Scott. What's the message?" Abby's voice filtered back into his awareness.

His racing heart sent shards of pain through his chest and his limbs shook. He tried to talk but couldn't control the stuttering.

Abby grabbed him by the arm and shook him. "Scott!" she screamed.

Raising her voice seemed to have the desired effect. He snapped out of his trance and stared at her before focusing on the screen again.

"Um... Um... I don't think I can handle this anymore."

Abby faced him and grabbed him by both arms. She stared hard into his eyes, the softness replaced by a steely glare. "Don't you give up now! I already picked you up out of the gutter once when you lost your family. I'm not gonna stand around and watch you slip into that dark hole again. You've got everything to fight for."

Abby's words were sharp, direct, and forceful.

"You couldn't stop what happened to Tina and Becky, but you can fight until your last bloody breath to save Cara and your baby. Don't you dare give up. Every single officer is fighting to find her. If you give up now, you're letting them all down – and yourself. Could you look at yourself in the mirror ever again?" Abby knew she had crossed the line in her fight to keep Scott in the game. He was a man she looked up to. Admired. Respected. And loved. She knew she had to do anything to keep her friend focused.

Scott stared straight ahead and took a deep breath. His eyes widened, as if he'd been in a boxing ring and his trainer had stuck smelling salts up his nose. He looked down at the screen and read the message.

It's time to play Russian Roulette. You have a choice of two locations. One will help you find Cara. The other is a dead end. Are you a betting man, Scott?

The entrance to the Memorial Gardens, Hove Cemetery. Or the information point at the Whitehawk Hill Nature Reserve.

There's a phone at each location within a Sainsbury's carrier bag. Easy to spot really. Both phones have only

*an hour's charge left. Your next clue is contained within a
message on one of those phones. Take your pick.*

*Come alone. If I see another police officer close by, Cara
drowns.*

Scott and Abby stared at each other for a few moments.
Then, he handed the phone to Abby. She read the message
in silence, mouthing the words.

"I can't be at both," Scott said. "They are at opposite ends
of the town. I'll never make it to both before they run out of
charge. He's picked another cemetery again," he hissed and
closed his eyes.

"We'll do this together."

"Abby, did you not see what he said? It's in the message.
He said... come... alone."

Abby shook her head and got up. "And you will. I'll go to
the Hove location. You head to the Whitehawk one. We'll
keep in touch by radio and earpiece. I'll go via the station
and get Mike to take me there but drop me off a few hundred
yards away. It sounds like he's got more of those wildlife
cameras set up to capture your movements."

Abby was already thundering down the stairs. She
continued to explain her plan to Scott who followed behind.

"I'll grab a change of clothes. I've got a pair of jeans, a
hoodie, and a baseball cap in my locker. Even if he's seen me
before, I can disguise my appearance. I'll pick up flowers on
the way so that when I arrive at the cemetery, it will look like
I'm coming to pay my respects. Hopefully I'll be able to spot
the Sainsbury's bag and radio you right away."

Abby paused for a moment by her car. "Do you want to
tell the boss? He needs to know."

Scott shook his head. "No. I'm done playing by the rules. By the time I speak to Meadows and endure one of his lectures, an hour will have passed. It would be too late by then. Besides, he'll want to get a helicopter from the National Police Air Service up in the air, have ground units stationed close by, and mount a full surveillance operation. There is no time for that."

He headed towards his car, giving the armed officers across the road in their unmarked car a small nod.

40

Scott screeched to a halt in a small car park that served the nature reserve. The information point was a short walk away. There were few cars in the car park at this time of day. Scott noticed a few dog walkers enjoying the lush green landscape.

He got out and took a moment to scan his surroundings, looking for anything that stood out. A solitary observer was off in the distance. A lone individual was parked in a car farther up the road in the direction from where he'd come. Perhaps someone with a pair of binoculars was pretending to watch the protected bird species that called this ancient landscape home.

Nothing he could see stood out as looking suspicious. At any other time he would have welcomed an opportunity to walk around here. The city called it their "vital green lung" because it provided the perfect habitat for grazing sheep, protected birds like the Dartford warbler, and rare native bees like the brown-banded carder bee. On this occasion, his visit carried a life-or-death conclusion, meaning he couldn't hang around.

He hurried along to the information point, a small hut which appeared to be closed. He peered in through the window. It had a counter with an array of posters around it, and information leaflets in plastic wallets stacked against one wall.

Scott stepped back and looked around, not seeing an orange Sainsbury's shopping bag in view. A litter bin close by grabbed his attention. He ran over to it and peered inside, thinking that the perpetrator may have used his bin strategy again. Other than discarded coffee cups, crisp packets, and black poop sacks, there was no evidence of the Sainsbury's bag.

Scott's patience started to wear thin. The rolling hills around him provided more vantage points than he could cover. A crop of trees close by piqued his interest. He made his way over to them, wondering if the perpetrator had fixed one of his cameras there. Looking up into the branches, he saw nothing from where he stood. This was turning into a fruitless exercise which only angered him further. He made his way around the hut and stomped around in the gorse. *Perhaps the bag was stuffed out of sight?* That didn't sit right with Scott. The message stated that it would be easy to spot.

Grabbing his phone from his inside pocket, he dialled Mike's number. It took a few moments before his call connected.

"Guv? Any joy?"

"Nope. I'm still looking. How are you getting on? Have you dropped off Abby?" Scott asked, checking the time on his phone.

"Yes, guv. I dropped her off about fifteen minutes ago.

She made the rest of the way on foot. I'm parked about half a mile away, down a side turning and out of sight."

"Okay, Mike. Stay alert. I'll touch base with Abby now." Scott ended the call and grabbed his radio.

"Abby, anything?" Scott asked after pressing on the mic button.

"Nothing so far, Scott," Abby whispered. "I'm at the entrance to the Memorial Gardens but can't see a Sainsbury's bag anywhere. There's a car park next door. I've checked and it's empty. I've not even seen a groundsman. It's deathly quiet. Stay on the line. I'm going to have a wander. I need to find somewhere to lay these flowers, in case I'm being watched."

"Okay," Scott said. He heard Abby's heavy breathing as she moved around the stones.

After spending the next few minutes poking around the graves, Abby felt something wasn't right for many reasons. It was too quiet. Other than the distant hum of traffic from surrounding streets, she heard nothing else. No breeze to rustle the leaves on the ground. No chirping birds. Not even the sound of a plane passing overhead. It was... literally deathly quiet. Many of the stone faces had eroded over time, the names of those who rested just a few feet below the ground barely legible. Dates throughout the ages surrounded her. 1947. 1962. 1959. 1974. 1935. Names etched in stone fitted those eras. Doreen. Kenneth. Jean. Joan. Ronald.

"I've not found anything, Scott. Have you?"

"Nope. I'm still looking. He's playing games with us."

"I think you're right. He's led us on a wild goose chase," Abby said on a sigh.

"That's where you're wrong," said someone behind her.

41

Abby spun round and came face to face with a man brandishing a knife just a few feet from her.

She stepped back to put distance between her and the man. He looked like an ordinary middle-aged man, dressed in jeans, an open-neck shirt, and a quilted Barbour jacket.

"Keep your distance. I'm a police officer," Abby shouted, putting a hand out in front of her.

"I know." The man nodded. "You are Detective Sergeant Abby Trent. Baker's sergeant."

Scott could hear the exchange as he listened in on her open mic.

"Abby!" Scott shouted, as he ran back towards his car. "Get away from him! Run!"

She didn't respond.

"I was hoping to get you alone," the man said. "I followed you all the way from Scott's house to the station. And I was prepared to wait there all day until you left. But I had a hunch that you would do whatever you could to help Scott through his latest challenge."

"So you followed me here?"

The man nodded and smiled. "And I know you were dropped off, choosing to make the rest of the journey on foot. Clever but not that clever." The man lunged at Abby with the blade.

She turned and ran, weaving through the gravestones, heading back towards the main road. "He's here, Scott! He's got a knife!" Abby screamed, as she reached into her bag to press the red emergency button on her radio.

Too quick for her, the man shoved her from behind. Abby tripped over her feet and fell forward, her hands outstretched. The palms of her hands scorched with pain as they grazed the tarmac path. As she scrambled to her feet, the man pushed her to the ground again. Abby's radio slipped from her grip and clattered to the ground. The heavy weight of the man landing on her back pushed the wind from her chest.

The cold steel of the blade pressed into her neck. She squirmed and kicked, bringing her elbow up to thrust it backwards. It connected with the side of the man's head which forced him to loosen his grip on her, but he pushed back down again.

"You try that again and I'll cut your throat from ear-to-ear. They won't have far to bury you," he hissed, pressing his mouth against her ear. "My issue isn't with you. Do as I say and I won't harm you. It's Scott Baker that I want. I'm sure you want to see your kids again."

He growled as he rose and grabbed Abby by her hair, pulling her to her feet. He kept one arm wrapped around her neck whilst keeping the edge of the blade pressed against her skin.

Abby complied, not wanting to inflame the situation further. With her radio on the ground somewhere behind her, and the contents of a handbag scattered, she had no way of reaching the others. She had to bide her time.

He guided her at knifepoint to beyond the car park and past a treeline which opened into a small clearing and a parked car. Abby looked around. There was no one walking, no vehicles passing, and no sign of help. Mike was just minutes away and oblivious to what was happening.

She tried to wriggle from the man's grip, gauging how much effort it would take to disarm him. She'd learnt many close-quarter safety procedures as part of her regular officer safety training. But without knowing the man's mental state and what he was capable of, she was treading a fine line. If she moved too slowly with a six-inch blade pressed into the small of her back, there was a real risk of harm.

The man guided her to the back of his car and popped open the boot before telling her to get in. Abby hesitated for a moment, her hands held high in a sign of surrender. She hoped it would calm his fears about the risk of retaliation.

"Get in," he demanded.

Abby stood her ground and stared into the darkened space of the boot. He still had his arm wrapped around her neck.

She thought about sinking her teeth into his arm but doubted it would have much of an impact through the quilted fabric of his jacket. The man took the decision from her when he shoved her with such force that she lifted off her feet.

Abby fell headfirst into the space, clipping her forehead on the rear bulkhead. Her vision blurred as a throbbing pain erupted. A wave of dizziness washed over her, followed by a sudden tingling dampness. White dots speckled her vision. Everything went dark after that.

———————

42

Through heavy breaths, Scott relayed the events to Mike as he raced along the seafront towards Hove. Blue lights flashed in sequence from the grille of his car and the siren wailed, warning others to make way. Having instructed Mike to get to the scene as soon as possible, he radioed through to Control to organise extra officers.

Dread filled Scott's mind as he willed the traffic to move faster. He wanted to speed up time so he could be there right now. With every minute that passed, the chances of finding Abby slipped further away. Minutes later he pulled up outside the cemetery. A small convoy of police cars filled the road, parked up on the pavement, their occupants already on the ground and searching the area.

Scott slammed his car door shut and ran to the entrance of the Memorial Gardens where Mike stood barking further instructions. Mike looked as worried as Scott.

"Any sign of her?" Scott asked, as his eyes shot in all directions, willing for one officer to shout that they had found her. He knew the shit storm that faced him back at the station. Scott had crossed the line and put a colleague in danger. He could only imagine what Meadows would say.

Mike shook his head and pursed his lips, leading Scott over to where Abby's belongings lay scattered on the ground. A blue-and-white police cordon tape remained in place around the scene to keep it sterile. Scott stood at the boundary and stared at the ground ahead of him. Abby's handbag lay with its contents spilled – a hairbrush, lipstick, a notepad, phone, several pens, and a pack of tissues. Her radio was farther away.

Scott watched as officers hurried between the lines of gravestones searching for evidence of Abby's presence, or worse, her dead body.

A few minutes passed before another officer jogged over to Mike and Scott. "Guv, there's a car park next door. Beyond it, and through the trees, is a small clearing with evidence of tyre tracks in the earth. Recent by the looks of it. There's also a trail of footprints that lead to the tyre tracks and what appear to be scuff marks. We've cordoned off the area. Shall I call in SOCO?"

Scott nodded before asking Mike to join him. They darted through the trees. The space opened up into a rough clearing. Not a designated car park, but a small piece of land skirted by trees which was being used as an overflow car park.

Scott stared at the ground as his mind played out the scene. He imagined Abby being forced against her will to get into a car. Scuff marks in the earth suggested that she may have put up a fight, but if her assailant had been carrying a knife, then she would not have antagonised him too much. Their training taught them to defuse situations rather than escalate them, whilst remaining calm and engaging in dialogue.

"Any witnesses?"

"No one that we've come across so far, guv. I've organised officers to spread out along the street but there are no residential properties for some distance either side. It's a vast area."

"That's why he chose it. He keeps outsmarting us at every opportunity. Can you inform the officers to search for any camera traps? He does things in a certain way. Nearly every location we've been to has had camera traps monitoring our movements." Scott looked around at the abundance of trees and overgrown bushes. Perfect hiding spots, in Scott's mind. "The bastard is probably watching us right now."

Ongoing reports from the officers conducting the search of the grounds didn't fill Scott with any confidence. Other than her belongings, nothing else suggested that Abby was being held within the grounds. The chopping of rotor blades above him signalled air support. With their thermal imaging cameras, they could search the grounds for any heat sources in areas that officers on the ground hadn't covered so far. Scott looked up and watched as the helicopter swooped from one side to another, sometimes hovering over a certain spot before moving on again.

Whenever an officer was in danger, they threw every available resource into the search. A dog unit arrived along with a dozen officers, with more arriving as each minute passed.

"Was there any evidence of her job phone? Or did she leave it at the office?" Scott asked.

Mike shrugged a shoulder. "If she had a job phone with her, then we've not found it yet. You know what Abby is like.

Half the time she either leaves it in the office or at home. Creature of habit. Prefers to use her own phone, and that's lying on the ground back there," he said, thumbing over his shoulder.

"Bollocks. How many times have I told her to keep both of them with her?" The sinking feeling continued to grow. They hadn't been able to make any inroads into tracking down Cara's location. Now they faced Abby suffering the same fate.

43

Moving Abby proved harder than he'd imagined. A dead weight. He dragged her from his boot, her feet thumping on the soil. After he lost his grip for a brief second, she crumpled in a pile on the floor.

"For fuck's sake." He hissed an exhale past his teeth.

Looping his arms under her armpits, he dragged her the few yards to the doors of the barn. The location was as remote and abandoned as the first. The one containing Cara was an old wooden structure. This was constructed of corrugated metal sheets. It was rusted, creaking, and pitted with tiny holes from years of corrosion, so perfect for him. Trails of weeds snaked up the sides of the barn trying to swallow it up.

He unlocked the padlock and pulled back the door; the hinges creaked in protest. The manufacturers of the Perspex vessel had eyed him with suspicion when they had delivered and installed his purchase. His fabricated story of the barn being cheap as chips and prime for being restored back to commercial use appeared to have been enough to convince them.

His intention had always been to kidnap both Cara and Abby. In his opinion, they were the two most important people in Scott's life. Abby was the only other person that he'd seen Scott spend considerable time alone with other than Cara. After months of surveillance, he'd witnessed the bond between Abby and Scott. The breakfasts, lunches, early morning runs, and laughter. He'd eavesdropped on their conversations in the coffee shop as they chewed over their lives and relationships. They appeared to share similar values, got on very well and were firm friends, as well as work colleagues.

To hurt Scott, he needed both women.

Once everything was in place, he'd left both structures alone for a few months, setting up camera traps to capture any unwanted attention. He'd needed to make sure that the locations were safe away from prying eyes, and would stay undisturbed.

The setup here was the same. A large Perspex vessel, the kind guests find brimming with exotic fishes in the lobby of exclusive hotels; a laptop with a live feed and an internet connection that transmitted his video through a complex network of hubs spanning the globe. He had done every-thing to cover his tracks as best as possible. It was the Perspex vessel that he admired the most. He'd gotten the idea after seeing images of a freestanding cylindrical aquarium called the AquaDom, a jaw-dropping spectacle in a Berlin hotel that contained a million litres of saltwater and one-thousand-five-hundred tropical fish.

His aquarium was a fraction of the size but suited his needs. Another pulley system hung from the roof struts.

Huffing and grunting, he blew out his cheeks as he dragged Abby's body towards the chair. Pulling her up into the seat, and with one hand pressed against her chest, he pushed her into place before securing her wrists to the sides of the chair with cable ties. He repeated the process with her ankles.

Abby's head tipped forward. He placed his fingers beneath her chin and tipped her head back. A one-inch cut on her forehead had streaked her face with blood. He slapped her cheeks. *Not too hard.*

"Wake up... Welcome to your new home." He shook her shoulders.

Abby groaned. Salty tears coated her eyelids as she blinked hard. Licking her lips, she looked around. It took a few moments for her brain to engage before her eyes widened. She stared at the man and yanked her arms, desperate to break free from the restraints. She winced as she looked down at her hands, the cable ties pressing hard into her skin.

"Detective... Sergeant... Abby... Trent. Understand I haven't got an issue with you. So don't make life hard for yourself. You're merely a pawn in my game. An opportunity to hurt Scott Baker even further."

Abby continued to wriggle in her chair, her teeth grinding, a guttural roar scorching her throat. "What do you hope to achieve by abducting a police officer?"

"To raise the stakes and bring Scott Baker to his knees."

Abby looked around, taking in her surroundings, searching for entry and exit points. "Where is Cara?"

He shook his head. "That's none of your business." He bowed his head for a moment, his own loss resurfacing. "But Scott Baker has to pay the price." He walked over to the chain and tugged at it.

Abby's chair lifted off the ground. Her own sharp intake of breath caught her by surprise; she looked at the floor and then above her. She gasped as her chair swung and inched towards the vessel.

"Enough! I'm a police officer. You don't have to make this any worse for yourself." Her words fell on deaf ears as her chair hovered over the vessel before being lowered into it. Her hands trembled and her stomach rolled. A sour taste filled her mouth, and she found it difficult to breathe.

Abby felt powerless. Years of training and her many years on the streets hadn't prepared her for anything like this. What she was being lowered into reminded her of the glass beakers she'd used in chemistry lessons as a teenager, except this one was a thousand times bigger.

Her feet touched the floor as the chair came to a rest.

This has to stop!" Abby screamed.

The man walked over to his laptop that sat propped up on a few wooden crates. He adjusted the lid of the laptop to make sure the camera feed was positioned correctly. After he tapped away on the keyboard, the live stream appeared on the screen. He nodded, happy with his work, then he walked back over to the vessel. He stared in silence, his eyes locked with Abby's.

"I won't be back. You won't see me again. Scott will have a choice to save you or Cara. I know you have a soft spot for him. Does he know that?"

Abby stared at him.

"I've seen you two nipping over to Munch for a coffee and a bite to eat."

She narrowed her eyes.

He nodded as the realisation dawned on her. "Yes, I watched you, Scott, and Cara dozens of times. I even sat in

Munch, a few feet from you both. You clearly value his friendship on many levels. I'm wondering if you mean enough to him, though?"

He relished every minute as he messed with her mind.

"The question is will Scott ever see you again?" He turned and walked out, locking the metal door behind him.

44

"You bloody fool!" Meadows bellowed, as he paced around his room. "Absolute fucking idiot. What were you thinking?" He jabbed his temple as he stared at Scott. "You went into a high-risk situation and placed yourself and a fellow officer at risk. The subsequent fallout from your negligence has resulted in Abby being abducted." Venom laced each word that Meadows spat out. "I've had the CC on the phone. Guess how that bloody went?"

Scott was desperate to continue his search for Abby. The guilt had crippled his thoughts as he'd scoured the grounds and surrounding treeline. But receiving a phone call from Meadows had curtailed his desperate efforts and sent him heading back to the station, just in time for this dressing down he didn't want or need.

As his boss continued to bluster, Scott sat with his hands in his lap, taking the barrage. He didn't blame Meadows for his reaction. There was nothing Scott could say that would vindicate his decision. But he had to try.

"I didn't expect it to go this way, sir. I'm sorry. I'm happy to speak to the CC directly if that helps?"

"No, Scott. You will not speak to the CC at all. This is a right shitshow. The CC is already demanding a full investigation into how one of his officers was abducted. This could cost both of us our jobs."

"Sir..."

Meadows leaned against the windowsill. "Shut up, Scott! My command of my team is under the spotlight. You made me look like an incompetent idiot." He took a long, deep breath and stared out of the window, as turmoil took over his mind. "The CC is drafting in another fifty officers to help in the search for Abby. We are already the talk of the force. Every single road leading to Hove cemetery is being searched. Every minute of CCTV along the route is being secured."

"I had no choice. It was a time-critical situation. He said that within an hour both phones would run out of charge. If I didn't act then, I would have been too late."

Meadows spun around and glared at Scott. "Why didn't you come to me first?"

"He said that if he saw another officer anywhere near either of the two locations, Cara would die. What would you have done differently?"

Meadows pulled his shoulders back, unhappy at being challenged. "For a start, a full risk assessment. Then agreed upon a plan of action and got it approved by senior officers. I would have sent teams of plain-clothes officers to conduct a surveillance sweep of both locations. If that threw nothing up, the officers would have been deployed at strategic points in around both locations, covering every conceivable route in order to lock down the situation at the first sign of trouble."

Scott stared Meadows in the eye. "And how long would that have taken? Would that have been delivered within an hour?"

Meadows stiffened and his eyelids twitched.

"Exactly," Scott said. "That's why I had to take the risk and act straightaway. If I came to you, a plan like you just suggested would have taken hours to organise and execute. Time wasn't on my side."

"And your plan worked, did it?" Meadows challenged.

Scott bowed his head. An uncomfortable silence lingered in the air between them.

Meadows dropped into his chair. "Now is not the time for this conversation. One of my officers is missing. Judging from the video feed that we've seen, the location where Cara is being held doesn't appear to have been used for a while." He leaned his elbows on the desk and formed a steeple with his fingers. "If I were him, I would have chosen a more remote location where he wouldn't be seen, especially based on how he's contained Cara in a glass tank. It's not the kind of thing you'd set up in your front lounge."

Scott nodded. "I agree with the remote location. The team have identified Sunray Tanks, a manufacturer in Somerset who specialises in this kind of thing. They ship all over the world to hotels and private customers. They're sending through details of fourteen orders in the last twelve months. Five are for customers in the UK."

Meadows picked up his phone. "Good. I'm going to request an NPAS unit to search the outskirts of Brighton and Hove. Maybe they can spot rundown and remote buildings that we can't see from the ground. They should be able to pick up any heat sources –"

Scott's phone bleeped, stopping Meadows in mid-flow. He grabbed it from his inside pocket. Another unknown number. Opening the message, he saw another web link, like the one he had received for Cara. He quickly glanced at the screen then looked at Meadows.

"It's a message from him."

Scott's grip on the phone tightened; he felt a quiver in his stomach and a slight chill race across his skin. An unshakeable sense of dread filled his thoughts.

Clicking on the link opened a live feed onscreen. He clenched his teeth when an image of Abby appeared. She was tied to a chair and appeared to be in a large glass tank similar to the one that Cara was being held in. He took a sharp intake of breath at the sight of the dried streaks of blood on her face.

"No..." Scott whispered, passing his phone to Meadows.

45

Pandemonium spread through the team when Scott raced into CID with Meadows hot on his heels. All eyes turned as Scott charged to the front and stopped by the incident board. He plugged his phone into a cable attached to a monitor.

"Gather around, team. If you haven't heard already, I received a live link that confirms Abby is being held by our suspect." He clicked on the link on his phone and watched as the feed appeared on the monitor. Officers were still gathering in small huddles around Scott. Several of them placed their hands over their mouths, horrified by the image. A few wiped tears from their eyes, whilst others looked away, distraught, shocked, and angered.

"Is she being held at the same location as Cara?" an officer asked.

"We can't confirm that at the moment. I've forwarded the link to Matt. His contact will now analyse the feed for its location, though I'm not hopeful because we could not find the source of Cara's feed." Scott examined the image before turning to his team. "My first impressions are that she is not being held in the same place. If you look at the background in each feed, they are different. They could be in adjoining buildings. We honestly don't know..." He shook his head.

As if she'd heard Scott's voice, Cara lifted her weary head and looked around, then she cried. The gathered officers watched in horror as the desperate scenes played out in real time. Abby thrashed around in her seat, frantic to break free from her restraints. Abby's suffering showed on her face; her features twisted with each tug she made on her wrists.

Scott wanted to jump through the screen and rescue both of them.

Feeling helpless standing there, he turned and barked instructions to his team. He wanted every available police informant turned over. Every crack house raided. All recent offenders released from prison to be re-interviewed again. Officers scurried to their desks knowing that every minute counted.

"Guv, we've not been able to find anything through our search of the area surrounding Hove cemetery," Mike said. "There isn't much we can do in terms of door-to-door searches, and the nearest premises are industrial or commercial which we'll check anyway. We've not uncovered any clues or confirmed any sightings. I wish we could do more."

Scott placed a hand on his shoulder. "I appreciate it, mate. I couldn't ask for any more from you or any other member of my team but get through that list of orders from Sunray Tanks as a priority. One of them could be from our suspect and the delivery details will help us to narrow down our search." He cast an eye around the room.

A broken man, Scott flitted between the desks, listening

in on the many conversations taking place. Several officers towards the back had congregated in a small group, coordinating a plan of action before they headed out to track down every informant on their books. About fifteen minutes later, Scott's phone rang again. Everyone fell silent and dozens of pairs of eyes turned towards him.

The number didn't register on caller ID, nor did he recognise it. But his sixth sense already told him who it was.

"Hello," Scott said as he answered the phone.

An empty silence greeted him. "Hello?" Scott said again.

"It hurts when you lose loved ones, doesn't it?" a voice replied.

This time the caller wasn't disguising his voice. The abductor was raising the stakes even further by taunting Scott. "Where is Abby?"

"That's for me to know. You're probably shocked that you can hear my voice clearly for the first time. That's because I'm not scared of you. You broke me. You broke me so badly that I lost everything."

Scott needed to keep the man talking. Meadows raced to the nearest phone to speak to Matt. Special software already rigged to Scott's phone recorded all incoming calls and messages.

"What did you lose?"

"I LOST EVERYTHING!" the man screamed down the phone.

For the very first time, Scott heard the man lose it.

He continued. "And now you're going to lose everything. I have the two most important women in your life. Their future rests in your hands. Decide who lives and who dies."

Panic gripped Scott and his throat tightened. His chest felt like a brick wall was crushing it.

"Listen... um..." Scott fought to make sense of the situation, his mind a blur of confusion and jumbled thoughts. He battled to find the right words. "It's me you want. Me. Not them. Me. Take me. Listen... Let them go. Please don't harm them. I'll meet you wherever you want. I'll come alone. Just promise me first that you will let them go."

Silence greeted him again. For a moment, Scott thought that perhaps his bargaining ploy was making the man consider his options.

"It doesn't work that way. This isn't over yet. Now the fun part begins. Watch the feeds."

A few minutes passed as Scott and the team glared at the screen. Nothing on either feed. Abby still thrashed in her chair. Cara sobbed.

There was an audible and collective gasp from the team when both Cara and Abby flinched in their seats and stared down at the ground. Their heads jerked from side to side as fear and panic spread across their faces. The sound of hissing came through the speakers on the monitor. The realisation hit Scott when water began to slowly seep into the bottom of the vessels.

"Watch them drown."

46

Officers stared at one another in disbelief and horror. Every single one of them had faced challenging, and sometimes life-threatening situations in the line of duty. None, however, had been abducted, paraded, or had faced an impossible situation where their colleagues were powerless to help them. Publicly they prayed for a positive outcome, but deep down, many felt utter despair. They bowed their heads knowing they could be watching the final few hours of two people close to their hearts.

Scott brought the phone up to his ear, not taking his eyes off the monitor for one second. "Why are you doing this?" he asked, weary resignation in his voice. "What happened to make you do something so extreme? You keep going on about having lost everything. I can't help or understand your situation unless I know what you've lost."

Scott looked at Meadows who circled his finger in the air, encouraging Scott to keep the conversation going.

The caller said, "You wouldn't understand. You didn't

understand back then. Everything that has happened in these last few days is completely your fault. I never wanted to do this. It's not in my nature. Never was. But ever since that day we crossed paths, my life changed. Because you *ruined* it!"

Scott heard a deep sadness in the man's voice. The anger that tinged his words moments ago had been replaced by despair and grief.

A pause. A hiss of breath. Another torturous second ticking by. Scott tried to keep the conversation going, but his questions failed to provoke a response. The oppressive atmosphere in the room cloaked everyone in tension. Shivers of fear tickled his back and his mind went blank.

"Drowning. It's an awful way to die, don't you think?" the caller said.

Scott didn't reply, still numb.

"Don't you think?" the man asked again.

"I guess."

"There's no guessing. It's a fact. Seeing a loved one drown stays with you forever. Affects people forever. And still takes lives. I felt that pain. You will too."

Scott paced up and down. He ran a hand through his hair and stared at the team. The look on their faces matched his feelings inside. "Who did you lose?"

"You lot must be shit at your jobs if you've not been able to figure that out. I don't want to do this. I need someone else to feel the pain that has riddled and infected my mind and body for so many years." He sniffed loudly. "There are days I can't look at myself in the mirror because I'm ashamed of who I've become. I didn't save and protect my loved ones. What kind of man does that make me? What kind of husband and father does that make me?"

Scott glanced at Meadows who wheeled both arms. By keeping the conversation going, they had their first crucial insights into the man. A husband and a father. Officers around Meadows dropped into their seats and tapped away on their keyboards. Every available online resource and police database was being scrutinised for cases linked to Scott and the information the abductor had just revealed.

"You said as a husband and a father.... What happened?" Scott asked.

"It doesn't matter now. If I see your officers anywhere near where Cara and Abby are being held, they will die instantly. There's a big oil drum filled with concrete suspended above each of them with a mechanism connected to the door. Any attempt to enter either building will release the drum, resulting in instant death." He paused for a moment then added, "In the next few hours both tanks will fill. The tanks are filling at the same speed, but it's unlikely that you'll find both of them in time."

"Please. Stop this now. Stop this before it goes too far," Scott pleaded.

"It's already gone too far. There's no turning back. You're on your own. I'm watching both locations remotely. Any sign of police nearby other than you will result in them dying. In the unlikely event that you find either location or both, who will you save?" The man paused for another moment. "Perhaps this time you'll be focused and not have your back turned at the critical moment when someone is drowning."

The line went dead.

47

S cott dropped his arms to his sides. As he did the phone fell from his hand and landed on the carpeted floor with a thud. The colour drained from his face; his eyes glazed over. A mixture of defeat and realisation had sucker-punched him, knocking all the fight from him.

Voices shouted around him, a mix of garbled messages that bounced from desk to desk. They sounded muffled, as if they were coming from another room. It felt like cotton wool filled his ears.

"Husband and father," Meadows shouted. "Someone closely connected to him that drowned. Search the whole of Scott's records," he barked as he marched over to Scott. "What happened?" Meadows grabbed him by the arms.

Scott staggered backwards. Helen appeared and grabbed one arm to steady him. Meadows wrapped an arm around Scott's waist to stop him from falling. Raj grabbed the nearest chair and shoved it in behind Scott's knees, forcing his boss to fold into the chair. Officers stood around, confusion, surprise, and concern etched on their features.

Scott's mind was in free fall as his subconscious dredged up memories that had remained firmly buried for years. His eyes darted from left to right and his lids flickered, as a sequence of images played like an old movie reel inside his mind.

Another officer knelt in front of Scott and handed him a glass of water. When he noticed the tremor in Scott's fingers, he promptly took it away.

"I... know what this is about." Scott's voice was even, quiet and broken.

Meadows shouted across the floor. "Has anyone got any information?"

Officers shrugged as they stared at their screens, many still trawling through years of Scott's history.

Helen crouched beside her boss and rubbed the back of his hand. "Guv, you're worrying us. Tell us."

"You can stop searching," Scott said, staring straight ahead, his eyes fixed on an imaginary spot somewhere in the distance. "Southend."

Helen furrowed her brow and glanced up at Meadows, who looked equally confused.

"Southend?" Helen prompted.

Scott nodded. "I couldn't save her. We weren't allowed. She was gone before I had the chance to do anything about it."

The room fell silent. Scott had everyone's attention. Meadows stepped back, nodding at Helen.

She squeezed Scott's hand. "What happened? Who couldn't you save?"

"Paul North is who you're looking for. His two-year-old

daughter, Phoebe, drowned when she slipped from his arms and fell from the pier into the sea. He begged me to jump in and save her. Pier staff held him back from jumping in after her. I was there with another officer, but I had my back to them when it happened."

Scott fell silent for a few moments, his lips moving silently as he recalled the events. "I was twenty-six years old and a probationer. Another officer and I were dealing with antisocial behaviour from a bunch of kids on the pier who were tossing chips at visitors. The first thing we knew of anything happening was when we heard a woman scream."

"What did you do to help?" Helen asked.

Scott hung his head. "There wasn't much we could do. I looked over the railings and there was no sign of her. There was a heavy swirl beneath us. She got swept away under the supports. We put in a call to the coastguard and to the lifeguards onshore. But that wasn't enough for Paul. He tried to scramble over the railings, but pier staff hung on to him. He begged me to jump in and save her. His wife was in bits. Paul was screaming. It was carnage. Dozens of members of the public were racing towards the railings to peer over, so there was a risk of one of them falling over the edge too. The sea temperature would have been enough to shock anyone unless they had the right equipment, clothing, or training. We could have had multiple casualties or worse. The pier is over a mile long and at least five metres deep at high tide." Scott sniffed and wiped his nose with the back of his sleeve.

"Then what happened?"

"I didn't know what I was doing. Everyone was shouting and screaming at us and the staff. It was against the force's health and safety guidelines. We were to not put ourselves in danger unless we'd had the right training."

Helen leaned in. "Of course you couldn't put yourself in danger too. You did the right thing."

Scott huffed. "I read those guidelines a million times after the incident. They're still etched in my mind." He stared up at the ceiling and mumbled off-key phrases. "Health and Safety – Water Safety – states: Essex Constabulary does not expect or require any member of staff to enter water in a rescue attempt of any person or animal under any circumstances. Rescuing members of the public or animals from water lies primarily with other emergency services that are equipped and trained to undertake such tasks."

"Right," Meadows said.

Scott shook his head. "But we were the emergency services. We were all they had. We were supposed to do a 'dynamic risk assessment', an on-the-spot judgement as to the likelihood of things going wrong. Everything had gone wrong already."

"It wasn't your fault, Scott. None of it was. Phoebe's father is wrong to blame you," Meadows said.

48

S cott rose from the chair, lurching and swaying before finding the strength to stand straight.

He turned to Meadows. "It doesn't feel like that. I know what it's like to lose a child. I blamed others when I lost Becky. It's only natural. He's doing the same. In his own twisted way, he's trying to get closure by seeing me suffer and take the fall. He wants me to hurt how he's been hurting for over twenty years. But why now, after all these years?"

An officer handed Meadows a printout of details they had recovered on Paul North. Meadows scanned the information before handing it to Scott. "Does the face look familiar?"

Scott stared down at the image and nodded. Paul North looked like a humble family man. Small metal-rimmed glasses, thin lips, large forehead with a receding hairline. He had kind features and looked as if he couldn't harm a fly.

After a sharp intake of breath, Scott stared at the angelic features of Phoebe North. A young child who hadn't started life properly. A toddler with a voracious appetite for exploration, mayhem, and mischief. Phoebe was the cheeky little daughter who was the apple of her father's eye. That was how they had described her during the coroner's inquest.

Scott felt sympathy for the man. He had harboured pain for over twenty years and hadn't come to terms with it.

Meadows rifled through a few more printouts. "Get local officers to attend his last known location," he shouted to no one in particular.

"Already done it," Mike shouted back. "The system hasn't been updated. He moved on from his last known address a year ago. Hopefully Essex Police have a better handle on his location." Mike tapped away on his computer.

He moved on from his last known address a year ago. About the same time he started following me and Cara.

"Shit," Meadows said, as he read the latest intelligence on Paul North. He looked up at Scott. "I think I know why he's done it now. His wife Coleen suffered depression after that tragedy. She was under the guidance of the Southend mental health unit for many years. Years of therapy and anti-depressants." He closed his eyes for a few moments and let out a deep sigh before continuing. "They tried to rebuild their lives again, had a son, and all was going as well as expected under the circumstances, but the grief and depression were too much for her. She took her own life eighteen months ago. An overdose. Sadly, she suffocated their twelve-year-old son, Billy, before killing herself."

Scott's chest heaved with anguish. The answer was there in black and white. He'd lost his family over the course of more than twenty years and losing his wife and remaining child had sent him over the edge.

Meadows marched to the front of the room. "Listen up, team. I want everything that you've got on Paul North. His latest movements, who his friends are, what he drives, who he banks with, mobile phone movements. We know he's been using lots of burner phones, but he must have a personal phone. If the GPS is on, or has been used in the last few days, we should be able to get the triangulation and cell site data."

"I'll speak to the DVLA and see if we can get an index for what he drives, and then I'll search ANPR records," an officer said, rushing back to his desk. Meadows nodded.

"Sir, I need to find him. It's me he wants," Scott said.

"I know but your life is in danger. You're not going anywhere within ten feet of him. Whenever you're out of this building you'll have a covert armed unit following your every move. I'm not jeopardising your safety. Understood?"

"Understood, sir." Scott appreciated Meadows's concern, but he couldn't sit on his arse whilst Cara and Abby were going through such horrific and harrowing experiences. He needed to slip his armed protection before Meadows had it authorised and in place.

Mike came and stood alongside Scott. "Guv, I need to see you in private," he whispered.

Scott furrowed his brow at Mike. "Yep, my office now."

He closed the door behind them and stuffed his hands in his pockets. "What's up, Mike?"

His officer handed him two printouts. Scott scanned the details. His eyes widened as he glanced at Mike who nodded. "Are you sure?"

"Not a hundred per cent, guv. It's not in her desk, and the current location isn't her home address. I've checked the order list from Sunray. The GPS location matches a delivery address not far from there. Let me follow this up?"

"We need to do this by the book. I should tell the boss,

but time is a critical factor here. Rather than swarming the area, why don't you do a recce? Do what they trained you to do in the army. It could save a lot of time, and if it's a credible threat, we can go public with Meadows. Understand?"

Mike headed for the door. "I'll go home and get changed and make my way there."

"Be careful, Mike. Don't put yourself at risk."

"Risk is my middle name, guv."

Scott paused in the doorway for a moment and placed a hand on his officer's shoulder. "Thanks, Mike, you're a good man."

He smiled. "True, but don't tell anyone. It could ruin my reputation."

Scott smiled as Mike shot off down the corridor.

Perhaps a glimmer of hope?

49

Scott stared around his office. It had been a while since he'd felt so alone. He heard the murmur of conversations filtering through from the main floor. His mind jumped all over the place. A part of him wanted to be with the team fighting to save the lives of Cara and Abby. Another part felt broken and lost.

An icy shiver of sadness prickled his skin as he leaned his head against the wall and closed his eyes, contemplating the pain of losing the two women who'd had the biggest impact on his life in recent years. He needed to keep going for them whatever the cost. He thumped the wall with the side of his fist, desperate to release the frustration that simmered beneath the surface.

"Scott."

He opened his eyes and glanced back at the door, unaware that Matt had stepped into his room.

"How are you holding up, mate?"

"I'm not. I'm just so... I don't know what I am. Angry? Sad? Scared? Any of the above," Scott replied with a shrug.

"I can't imagine how you're feeling. But I promise you we are doing everything we can. I should hope to hear from my *colleague* soon."

"Soon might be too late..."

Matt nodded, knowing nothing outside of a break-through in the case could reassure Scott. "I thought I'd give you an update on the video feed analysis and digital enhancement." He stood alongside Scott and held up a few photocopies taken from Abby's feed. "We've done our best to enhance the background without distorting the image. It's a fine line between securing the clarity and pixellating the image too much. If you look at this area..." Matt began, circling an area on the image with his finger, "it looks like an industrial unit. It's not flat metal sheets, it's corrugated."

Scott narrowed his eyes at the image. "An industrial unit?"

Matt grimaced. "More than likely. I'd say old. We've iden-tified significant deterioration and corrosion to the fabric of the building. There is hardly any clean metal from what we can see."

These insights gave Scott and his team the chance to focus their attention on likely locations.

"How did you get on with Cara's feed?"

Matt rummaged through a few sheets before pulling out the digital enhancements. "That's a completely different setup. From what we can tell, Cara's being held in something more dilapidated." Matt ran his finger along vertical grid lines on the printout. "We noticed what we believe to be gaps in the building's fabric. Daylight."

"Also a metal construction?"

"We can't be certain. Corrugated sheets can deteriorate so much that daylight can poke through. However, when they do rust over a lengthy period, pinprick holes appear and increase in size as the metal breaks down. I'd say this is a natural material. Wooden."

Scott processed the information and rubbed his temples. "So, you're suggesting that Abby is being held in a structure constructed of metal, whereas Cara is being held in something made of wood or ply?"

"Yes."

"Finding Abby's location might be easier than Cara's. North could be holding Cara prisoner in a huge bloody garden shed for all we know."

Scott thanked Matt and headed back to his team.

He made his way towards Raj's desk, grabbing Helen along the way. He updated them on Matt's findings. "I want you both to coordinate the search for industrial estates and distribution units, especially ones that might not be in use at the moment, perhaps expired leases?"

"We did a similar search a while back in another case," Raj said, wiggling his mouse to wake up his screen. He sifted through his records. "This is it. The last time I ran the search, the Brighton and Hove area had two industrial estates. One in Coldean and the other in Woodingdean. I remember there were a few units that were unoccupied."

"Worth checking again?" Helen asked.

Raj shrugged a shoulder. "Going on what the guv has said, I doubt it. They are both modern estates. Clean and shiny fabricated steel units. And they're busy. Nothing like what we are looking for."

Scott said, "Fair point, Raj. Send officers to double-check again. There might be old or abandoned buildings on the edge of those estates. A lot of open land surrounds them. There could be a disused building somewhere?"

"I'm going with the guv on this. Better to be safe than sorry," Helen said.

Raj leaned back in his chair and went with the majority. "There is another angle that we need to consider."

"Go on," Scott said.

"He's not left a digital or monetary footprint anywhere so far. If he had rented any commercial unit, regardless of its condition, he would have had to take out a lease. That would entail credit checks, deposits, monthly direct debits. I can't see him doing that. He's been too careful up to now. We can search these areas, but I think we need to focus on abandoned locations. I mean *really* abandoned locations."

Scott nodded and agreed. "It's the most likely place he could hold either Cara or Abby. We're looking at places that have been abandoned for years, if the digital enhancements are anything to go by."

"Exactly. Ruins," Raj added.

Scott reached for the nearest desk phone. He needed NPAS to send up a helicopter unit to search the surrounding countryside.

50

Scott returned to his office with Helen hot on his heels.

"Guv, where's Mike?"

He dropped into his chair and pulled out his phone. "He's out following up leads and will report in soon. Do you need him for anything?"

"No, guv. Nothing in particular. He was chasing down the phone companies, requesting cell site data on any numbers that were near Hove cemetery at the time of Abby's abduction. I wanted to know how he got on with that. Do you want me to follow up whilst he's not around?"

"No, you crack on with searching for the units with Raj and a few others."

Helen nodded and disappeared, leaving Scott to stare at his phone screen. He flicked between the two text messages containing the links. When the images appeared, he gritted his teeth, drawing on every ounce of strength to keep it together. His heart quickened when he looked at Cara. She was wet and shivering. She wriggled in her chair and stared around in despair. Cara would go through moments where she screamed, and each piercing cry stabbed Scott through the heart. The water, now up to her shins, was rising quicker than he'd expected.

Switching between the feeds, Abby was faring little better. She was more vocal and aggressive, shouting at the top of her voice, hoping someone would hear her, then tugging on her restraints. Frustration boiled over when an ear-piercing scream tore from her throat.

He dropped the phone on his desk and looked away. At the current rate, they would both drown in a matter of hours – if they didn't succumb to hypothermia first.

Numbers at the station swelled with a melting pot of officers from Sussex bases. Meadows had drafted in officers from Worthing, Newhaven, Burgess Hill, and Bognor. The boardroom, canteen and press room had all been commandeered to provide the extra space. The scale of the search was beyond anything Scott had ever seen.

With the CC on Meadows's back, a sense of urgency drove everything they did. A press release issued informed residents of Detective Sergeant Abby Trent's and Dr Cara Hall's disappearances. Members of the public were urged to come forward with any information or sightings that might help in the search for both women. North's details had also been released as a person of interest in their investigations. More lines had been installed to cope with the flood of calls.

His heart tugged at the thought of Abby's kids being made aware of their mother's situation. They were being cared for by relatives and a FLO, but Scott knew that would be little consolation.

A further hour passed as Scott sat, tapping his fingers on the desk. He'd checked the live feed several times, only to see the water level creeping towards their knees. With no word from North, the outlook didn't look good. Essex Police hadn't been able to confirm North's location. He was on their system as having no fixed address. Local officers had visited all known locations, friends and relatives associated with him.

Helen jolted Scott from his dazed state when she ran into his room. "NPAS has picked up a faint heat source in an old building three miles north of Lewes."

"What kind of heat source? Big enough to be a human?"

"More than likely. It's static and the map shows the building as being down a long dirt track, surrounded by fields. The nearest occupied building is a farm at least two miles away. The structure looks like an old wooden barn. It's partly obscured from the air by a canopy of trees, but from what they can see, it looks abandoned."

"Any vehicles in the area?"

Helen shook her head.

Scott jumped from his seat and grabbed his jacket. "I'm going to head there now. If anyone asks, you haven't seen me, okay?"

Helen bit her bottom lip and looked around nervously as she followed Scott out of his office. "Guv, I'm not sure that's a good idea. You know what the boss said."

Scott leaned in closer to Helen and spoke in a hushed tone. "I know what he said. I can't sit around and do nothing. This could be Cara. She's being held in a wooden building. What if it's her and we waited too long to get there?"

"I know. But you can't go there alone. Besides, your armed protection is waiting outside. The minute you leave this building, they'll follow. They won't let you go in there alone, will they?"

Scott had already thought of that. Despite going against every rule and regulation, he needed to do this alone. If North had set up camera traps, the presence of other officers could inflame the situation further. "I'm going to slip out the side exit. There wasn't space in the car park this morning, so my car is around the corner. I reckon I can get there without being spotted."

"Let me come with you?"

Scott smiled and placed a hand on Helen's arm. "I appreciate it, but I can't afford to get you in trouble as well. Abby is already in trouble because of me. I'm not prepared to put you in the firing line too. Just remember, if anyone asks, you haven't seen me. I'll phone you when I've checked the location. If it looks credible, you can call in the cavalry. Agreed?"

Helen took a long breath. Scott was putting her in a difficult situation, but she saw the pain etched on his features.

She said, "Disappear then."

51

As he sped out of Brighton heading east towards Lewes, Scott knew that a heat source could mean anything. It seemed ironic to him, as Sussex Police had their headquarters in Lewes. He tapped nervously on the steering wheel as he wove in and out of cars at speed.

A pressing need to do something propelled him forward, even though he hadn't really thought it all through. He felt impotent sitting around waiting for news, so he had to do everything within his power to save Cara and Abby. If anything were to happen to either of them, he doubted he could survive the guilt on top of that already existing within him.

Entering the outskirts of Lewes, he took the A275 north, and raced through the leafy town, before leaving it in his rear-view mirror to continue his journey. He pulled over in Cooksbridge, a small Sussex village, and checked his bearings again before taking a sharp left towards a location given by the NPAS unit.

With just a hundred yards left, Scott pulled over onto the

verge and parked up. If North had the building under surveillance, he wanted to approach unnoticed to give him as much time as possible. Scott checked Google Maps on his phone, confirmed the direction and set off, pushing his way through the hedgerow. Bramble and branches snagged on his clothes; He gritted his teeth and shoved them aside.

Dropping into the field on the other side, he jogged along the perimeter, keeping low and scanning his environment. Deathly silence surrounded him. He prayed it wasn't an omen for what was about to come. His heart hammered in his chest and his pulse throbbed in his neck as he slowed and crouched.

Up ahead and on the other side of the boundary, he spotted the old wooden barn obscured from above by a canopy of trees, as described by the air unit. Scott crept along, listening for any signs of movement as he stared at the barn. If North was being true to his word and the front door was rigged, he couldn't risk entering from that direction. Besides, if this was a credible location, then North would have set up a camera trap to alert him to any intruders. He needed to enter from the rear, where his approach would be hidden from view.

Twigs snapped beneath his feet as he came to a small gap in the hedgerow, barely big enough for him to squeeze through. But it would have to do. He swore when loose branches snapped back and slapped him in the face.

He stared at the dilapidated barn. Weathered, worn, and beyond repair in his opinion. He imagined it hadn't been used in at least twenty years. *Storage for grain in years gone by.*

Scott got out his phone and updated Helen before he continued his approach. He held his breath as he made his way towards the rear of the structure. Once there, he exhaled. He pressed his ear against the wooden slats. There was silence. No sound of running water, no cries or screams.

Scott inched along the wall searching for any signs of a loose board, or a knot that had dried and fallen out, offering him a convenient eyehole. It didn't take him long to find a few loose wooden planks that were clinging to the fabric of the building by a few rusty nails. He didn't want to break them off for fear of making too much noise, so Scott eased them to one side. It took a bit of persuasion and patience. Both of which he was running out of. Having created a small opening, he peered inside the dark space. His view was obscured by old machinery and rotting hay bales.

He rolled onto his side, squeezed through the gap, and paused.

A slither of dread pricked his skin. *This doesn't feel right. Something is wrong.*

Everything Scott imagined he would see didn't appear. There was no glass vessel. No Cara. No Abby. Just emptiness. A dark, dusty space. He got to his feet and looked around. There was indeed old machinery and hay bales to his left. The rest of the space was empty.

A dead end.

A sinking feeling swamped Scott and his shoulders dropped. He reached for his phone and was about to text Helen with an update when he heard a rustling behind him. He spun round. His eyes widened and his breath caught in his throat. He raised his fists, ready to defend himself, and took a step back.

"What the bloody hell? Who the fuck are you?" came a hoarse and gravelly voice.

Startled, Scott backed up even farther. A dishevelled figure rose from the bed of hay. A tramp. The man moved and released a stench of stale sweat that drifted in Scott's direction and soon tickled his nose.

"I'm the police. Who are you?"

"I live here," the old man replied.

Scott put the man in his early sixties. An old, tatty coat peppered with holes was tied at the waist by cord. Trousers – if you could call them that – hung on his thin frame, stained and faded. Scott wondered how old they were. He glanced down at the man's shoes. The stitching barely held them together, and a big toe poked out of one of them.

Scott breathed a sigh of relief when he realised he wasn't in danger. But disappointment soon replaced the adrenaline that coursed through his veins.

52

"False alarm," Scott bellowed into his phone, as he paced around his car. With the signal dipping in and out, he was having a hard time being heard.

"Yes, false alarm," he repeated. He glared at the screen and saw the signal bars tumble to nothing. "Fucking signal," he growled, and tossed the phone onto the roof of his car.

He leaned against the door. *Now what?*

Not having heard from Paul North bothered him. The man had been keen on taunting Scott at every opportunity, but since his last threat, all communications had stopped. He'd worked through all the burner numbers without success.

Scott checked the horizon seeing nothing but trees, fields, and hedgerows. The scale of the search was too huge. Meadows could have five hundred officers scouring Sussex and it wouldn't make any difference. The unsettling thought that Cara and Abby were being held farther afield crossed Scott's mind, but he quickly pushed it aside.

His phone rang and rattled across his roof. He glanced at

the screen, barely one bar. Matt was trying to get through to him.

"Hello, Matt. Can you hear me?" Scott asked. There was silence at the other end. It took a few moments before he heard Matt's voice and a few words dotted between lengthy periods of silence. The location was proving dreadful for keeping in touch with anyone. He paced around the track, waving his phone in the air whilst checking the screen.

Two bars! Nope, one bar. Bollocks. Yesss. Two bars again.

"Matt, can you hear me?"

"Barely. Shitty reception. Where are you? I've been trying to get hold of you urgently. I asked Helen where you were, but she didn't know."

"Yeah sorry, mate, I'm in the arse end of nowhere following up on a lead. Bit of a dead end in terms of the lead and phone signal."

"Don't worry about that. I think I might have a location for you on Cara's feed. The information on Abby's feed will be with me in the next ten minutes."

Scott sighed. He couldn't face the possibility of another dead end.

"I heard from my former colleague a few minutes ago. We've got a result. The friend of a friend analysed the feed for us. He put in a backdoor code when there was a lapse in security."

"How?"

"I don't know the ins and outs myself. However, what I am led to believe is that one node hidden behind the Tor must have gone down for a brief moment, which made the feed visible and traceable for a few seconds before it was cloaked again. He'd set up an alert on that feed for any outages. Their guess is that the node must have frozen and needed rebooting. In that brief window when it was exposed, he planted a tracking code."

Scott felt a surge of renewed energy rush through him. This was the break he had been waiting for. He clenched a fist in excitement. "Where does that leave us?"

"It revealed a complicated network of independent nodes scattered around the globe. His feed is running through over ninety locations in sixty-two countries, to disguise its identity and make it untraceable. There was only one IP address connected to a node on UK soil for this feed. That's where the laptop will transmit from."

"Shit, have we got a location?" Scott asked.

"Pretty much. From what I can see on Google Maps, there's a building on the eastern flank of Clayton, off Under-hill Lane. It appears as if the feed starts its journey from somewhere around there."

Scott tried to check the location on his phone but fumed when his screen froze whilst downloading a map. "Matt, I think I'm about fifteen to twenty minutes away from that location. I'm going to head there now. Can you tell Raj and Helen to make their way there and let Meadows know? He'll probably hit the roof when he knows I'm heading there solo, but we really don't have any time to waste."

"Will do. Scott, be careful."

"Always. One other thing, make sure Meadows gives the instruction that all officers are to stay a safe distance back and out of view until they hear from me." He jumped back in his car and sped off to the new location.

53

A single lane track with dense side verges slowed Scott's progress to the new location. Occasional breaks in the greenery confirmed the remoteness. Fields spread as far as the eye could see. He checked his phone to make sure he was close. It didn't help that once again his phone signal kept disappearing.

Knowing that he was just a few hundred yards away, Scott pulled up in a small access lay-by and parked up, deciding to make the rest of the journey on foot. Branches from unkempt trees formed a natural canopy that shielded him from view. Deciding on the direction, he set off whilst checking his phone. He needed to have a signal to check the live feeds.

When there was a clearing, his signal bounced back to full strength. Taking one such opportunity, he stopped and checked on Cara and Abby. The water was surging in at an alarming rate, past their waists and inching up towards their chests. Both Cara and Abby were screaming, battling with their restraints, and crying. Panic tore from their throats and drilled into Scott with deafening accuracy.

This wasn't going the way he'd planned. *But what did I plan for anyway?* He was running around the countryside playing to North's tune.

Since the first envelope and the first voice message, North had been calling the shots. This wasn't a spur-of-the-moment act of vengeance. North had planned for this moment over the course of a year. Grief had turned to revenge. He'd tracked Scott's movements, parked up in his street, and spied on him many times, and trailed him whilst he'd shared special moments with Cara. Now all of those months of watching, planning and plotting were culminating in a few days of utter revenge and destruction.

He'd felt sympathy for the man to begin with. After all, he'd lost his whole family, but when it had become personal, Scott's only focus now was to save the women he cared about. He didn't care whether North lived or died because of his actions. That was his choice.

He fired a text to Mike for an update. A few seconds later he received a reply.

Lost the signal. Know location. Will continue.

"Shit."

His walk turned into a light jog. Time wasn't on his side.

54

Sweat prickled his forehead and adrenaline tensed his muscles. Scott stopped in mid-step and spotted a wooden building to his left, covered in green moss and ivy. He inched closer, keeping low, and tucked into the hedge. He scanned his surroundings, looking for signs of anyone else. Scott wondered if North was watching from a distance or relying on a camera trap to alert him of any unwanted visitors.

He was just a few feet away when he heard a blood-curdling scream. One he would never forget. It was a life-threatening cry for help from a woman in despair.

His body stiffened. Every sinew of his being wanted to charge in, but he needed to approach with caution, so he made his way towards the rear of the barn, scanning the trees for camera traps. Much like the previous one, this building was in a state of disrepair. The march of time and nature had consumed the structure. Weeds and trails of ivy snaked across its fabric, attempting to claim it.

Scott stopped near two wooden slats and pushed them apart.

His eyes widened when he peered inside and spotted the glass vessel in the gloom with Cara inside it, strapped to the chair. He glanced up and noticed the barrel of concrete hanging above her. A cable, strung across the rafters, was attached to the front door. He couldn't see the locking mechanism or how the barrel would be released, but the threat was real.

Scott reached for his phone. *Thankfully one bar.*

He sent Helen a text to confirm he'd found Cara and needed backup at once. He pushed the slats aside and wriggled through the tight space.

Cara looked over her shoulder when rays of light poked through and caught her attention. Her eyes widened.

Scott placed a finger to his lips so North wouldn't be tipped off about his arrival.

Her expression softened in response. She looked on, tears tightening her face.

He looked beyond Cara and spotted the laptop perched upon some beer crates. He circled around the edge of the barn towards the device and out of camera view, and closed the lid.

He ran across to the cylinder and banged on it. It wasn't glass as expected. It had a slight flex. *Perspex or acrylic.*

"I'm getting you out. You're going to be okay," Scott shouted, holding up his hands to calm her. He ran around the edge of the vessel, scanning its base and top edge, looking for a drain plug to release the water.

"Please, Scott. Hurry. I don't want to die!" Cara shouted through her tears, as the water worked its way towards her neck.

"You're not going to die. I won't let you die," Scott said. He punched and shoulder-charged the vessel. It was too thick and strong for him to do anything.

"It looks like poor Abby is going to drown!" came a voice through the speaker on the laptop.

Scott glanced around. He found a second camera installed into a recess above the door. He ignored it, not caring that the man was watching his desperate attempts to save Cara.

Cara's eyes widened as the realisation hit her. "No! No! Not Abby as well?"

Scott glanced at Cara and nodded.

The water was rushing in at such a rate that Cara would drown in minutes if he didn't do something now. The water was entering from a valve set into the base of the tank, but he couldn't find the pipe leading to it. He glanced down at the ground. Nothing. *It must be buried.*

"Scott, you've got to save Abby as well," Cara shouted.

"I know," he shouted back.

Nothing in the barn would help him scale the tank. No ladder or chair, only a crude chain and pulley system. Scott figured it had been used to place Cara in the tank. It was locked in place with a padlock. *Shit.*

He stared at Cara through the Perspex. She stared back at him. There were unspoken words of regret. Tears spilled from his eyes when Cara mouthed the words, "I love you."

55

"You're not going to get your revenge," Scott shouted. He didn't know whether North could hear him, but Scott would not let Cara die.

"So you chose Cara over Abby. You'll have to live with that decision for the rest of your life," North replied.

"Not if I have anything to do with it. If you wanted revenge, then you would have showed your face by now. I'm here," Scott said, thrusting his arms out by his sides. "Come and get me. I'm unarmed. I have no backup. One-to-one, you and me."

North didn't reply.

Scott's mind was in pieces. He continued to search around for anything he could scrape the ground with but saw nothing other than a few empty Coke cans. Scott grabbed two of them and stood on both, to flatten them. He raced around to where the compacted earth appeared to be fresher than the rest of the dirty ground.

Using both cans as improvised shovels, he scraped away at the ground. As his hands moved at a furious pace, the dirt sprayed in all directions. The tips of his fingers sliced open when they caught on the rough edges of the cans.

Every few seconds he shot Cara a look of steely determination. The water was lapping around her neck. She gasped with every breath, her body shaking with cold water shock.

Scott pushed harder with the tools, clawing at the soil. The muscles in his fingers ached, his teeth hurt from gritting so hard, and sweat dripped from his forehead. *I'm not going to let you die.*

Time seemed to slow. Minutes felt like hours as he continued to scrape away the soil, blackened from years of use and neglect. He grunted and groaned his muscles seized. Exhaustion hit him hard, but he pushed on until his fingers hit a solid object.

He looked down. He must have dug eight to ten inches. He'd hit a blue plastic pipe. *Yes! The water feed.*

He continued to claw the soil at a frenetic pace, pushing mounds of dirt away until a small gap appeared beneath the pipe. He wrapped his bloodied fingers under the pipe and took a firm hold before giving a firm tug.

It held.

Scott jumped to his feet and crouched before grabbing the pipe again and leaning back with all his might. It wouldn't shift.

"I will not give up," Scott growled with such intensity, it felt as if he'd swallowed a thousand razor blades. He gripped the pipe again and gave it a hard, fast tug with all the energy he could muster. It moved a little.

Or did it? Did I imagine it because I want it to be true?

With steely determination, he kept tugging hard and fast in short bursts. Without warning the pipe gave way, sending Scott sprawling on his backside with a heavy thud. It knocked the wind out of him. A spray of water hit him when the pipe fell loose. It spilled out over the ground.

Scott rolled onto his knees. The hole he had dug filled with water under pressure from the tank. He didn't have time to celebrate. He staggered to his feet exhausted and in pain. He needed to get in the tank.

The water had stopped halfway up Cara's neck, but she continued to scream to be let loose. Scott turned towards the laptop, not sure why, but something deep within him willed him to do it.

Beer crates.

He shoved the laptop to the ground, not caring whether North could see or hear anything, and grabbed both beer crates. Scott ran back to the vessel. Stacking one upon the other gave him an extra two feet of height. It left about a foot between the top of his head and the rim of the vessel, just enough for him to get a firm hold and pull himself up over the lip.

He gripped the edges but the strength in his fingers failed him. They were bruised, bleeding, and sore from digging. Each time he tried to grab the lip of the vessel, a cramp set in. He shook his hands to push away the cramp before trying one last time.

Pulling himself up, he used his feet to climb the sides of the vessel before hauling himself over the edge and tumbling over the other side. The water cushioned his fall for a few seconds. The shock of the water hitting his body jolted his senses and took his breath away. He dragged himself upright and waded towards Cara.

"I'm here, I'm here," he said, wrapping his arms around her. She cried into his chest. Deep, guttural cries shook her body. "It's over. You're safe now." He pushed his hands into the water and jammed his fingers into the cable ties, wrenching them apart. Each tie punished his already mangled fingers.

Cara tried to stand, but she screamed and dropped back into her chair when her joints seized up. Her body felt cold and numb. But at least she was free. The water level dropped as it poured from the excavated hole and flooded the floor.

Scott held Cara tight, not wanting to let her go ever again.

56

"You think you've won?" North said, as he stepped into the barn using the hole that Scott had created. He gripped a hammer in one hand, pointing it at Scott. "You think you saved her and yourself?"

Scott spun round to face North lurking in the shadows. It was the first time he had seen the man in person since that fateful day on Southend Pier. He was bigger built than Scott remembered. The North he remembered had been a puny figure, with a thin neck and sunken cheeks, framed with metal-rimmed glasses. But his kind face had been replaced with stony features. His cold eyes looked as if the light had been sucked from them.

Scott waded through the water and stood between North and Cara, blocking her from view. "This has to stop now. This ends here. Police reinforcements will be here within minutes. There is nowhere for you to hide. Put the hammer down and we can talk about this."

North sniggered and jabbed the hammer at Scott. "You're

hardly able to throw down demands. Look at where you are, and where I am. You're trapped with no escape."

Scott needed to keep North talking. He needed to buy time. "I still don't understand why you're doing this. I know you lost your family through a series of tragic events, but this isn't the way to mourn their loss. All you're causing is further heartache for yourself."

"I mourn their loss every day. I'm haunted by Phoebe's screams every day. How do you think I feel? Her screams echo inside my head during every waking moment and terrorise my dreams at night. I'm her father and there was nothing I could do to save her."

Scott nodded in understanding. "I feel your pain. I really do. But there was nothing we could do to save her."

"Yes, there was!" North screamed, his eyes sodden. "You were supposed to save her. You were part of the emergency services. That was an emergency, but you stood by and watched Phoebe disappear beneath the water and drown. You stood by and did nothing!"

"We couldn't risk anyone jumping into the water. The impact of jumping from such a height and the temperature of the water would have shocked anyone. Me, you, another bystander, anyone. We would have been dealing with multiple injuries and possibly further fatalities. They didn't train me in water rescues." Scott moved closer to the wall of the tank. "I was a probationer. It was all so new to me."

North rushed the vessel and slammed his hammer into the surface. A faint hairline surface crack appeared in it. Scott jumped back in shock. Cara screamed at the sudden noise. The twisted snarl on North's face made him look like a demented soul hell-bent on destruction.

Scott narrowed his eyes when the first sounds of a siren

carried on the wind. Relief washed over him.

"Give it up, North. It's over. You will have firearms officers pointing their guns at you within minutes. You don't want this to end badly."

North shook his head. "It doesn't matter to me. Let them put a bullet in my head. At least I'll be with my family. It was bad enough that you didn't save Phoebe. Your actions ultimately led to my wife taking her own life and that of my son. And all I've done for the last year is watch you play happy families with your new girlfriend. I've watched you sit with Cara smiling and laughing." North stepped back and glared at Scott. "Tell me what I have to smile and laugh about? Tell me one thing that is good in my life? Why should you get to carry on with life like nothing has happened?"

Scott pleaded, desperate to keep North talking. "I swear there was nothing I could do. This path of revenge that you've taken has only damaged you further. What could you possibly gain from it?"

North gritted his teeth. "What could I possibly gain? I'll tell you what. I've watched you suffer and experience just an ounce of the pain that I've felt for over twenty years. This isn't over." He backed away, looking over his shoulder.

The sirens grew louder and the distant sound of whipping helicopter blades filled the air.

"I knew I'd broken you when I sent you your dead wife's ring. But that's nothing compared to the pain you're about to feel. Where is the one place you feel the safest?" North asked, as he backed out of the hole and disappeared from view.

Scott raced forward and hammered his fists on the vessel.

"No!" he screamed.

57

Though it felt like hours, in a few minutes, officers poured through the hole that Scott had created in the back of the barn. Helen had briefed everyone about the barn door being rigged. Other officers smashed holes in the weak structure. Shards of light poked through, brightening the gloomy space.

Firearms officers, ambulance paramedics, and fire service personnel all descended on the barn. A cacophony of noise filled the small space as each new set of boots arrived.

Helen pushed through to the front, an abject look of fear on her face, as she placed both hands on the vessel. She looked between Scott and Cara. "Fuck."

"Get me out of here, quick. North has escaped and I know where he's going! He's heading to the cemetery. Get units on the ground there immediately," Scott shouted.

The minutes dragged by as fire service personnel rigged up a temporary ladder system to scale the wall of the vessel and attend to Cara.

Scott knelt by her side. "You're going to be okay now. I

need to go after him. I need to stop him."

Cara grabbed his hand. She saw the mix of pain and anger in his eyes. Every cell of her being wanted Scott to stay. To make her feel safe. But she could see the determination in his eyes, so she nodded her agreement.

Scott scaled the ladder and hauled himself over to the other side, assisted by firemen. Two paramedics waited on the ground as he stepped off.

"You need to get those looked at," one of the air ambulance paramedics said, pointing at Scott's bloodied hands.

Scott waved away their concern. "Later. Deal with Cara first. She needs immediate medical attention." He shouted to the officers gathered in the barn. "Has anyone spotted North?"

Blank faces greeted his question.

"Guv, leave this to the others. NPAS are on the way," Helen said. "ETA is nine minutes. They'll be able to scour the land far better from the air."

"He had a head start on us. He'll be long gone now," Scott replied.

He charged through the gap in the back of the barn and winced as bright daylight pierced his eyeballs.

Helen followed him out, grabbing him by the back of his jacket. "Guv, please. Cara needs you. Get yourself looked at first and I'll deploy more troops on the ground."

Scott stopped and turned to face Helen. He gave her a big hug. "Thank you for everything. And I mean everything. I couldn't have done this without you. North needs stopping. This is personal. I know where he's going, and I need to stop him." He ran for his car.

Helen raced after him. Tears filled her eyes. "Guv, Abby's feed. It's gone down."

58

Scott pulled away from the kerb, heading back to Brighton. He'd left Helen to oversee the scene and to make sure that Cara received emergency treatment before being transported to the hospital. His heart sank again as his mind took him back to the scene, and the look on Cara's face when he had discovered her. She'd looked broken and scared.

He slammed his palm on the steering wheel.

"Fuck!" He screamed with all his might, until his throat hurt.

Something out of his control had led to Cara and their unborn baby being put in a life-threatening situation. Guilt washed over him, smothering him until he had to gasp for breath.

Scott hit the button on the steering wheel and waited for his call to connect with Mike.

"Come on, come on..." He said with a groan, his impatience growing with each second that Mike didn't answer.

Did our plan backfire? Didn't Mike make it in time? An

uncomfortable thought crossed his mind. *Did Mike come to harm?*

Scott flinched when his Bluetooth speaker crackled into life.

"Guv..." Mike sounded out of breath.

"Did you get her?" Scott asked then held his breath. The line crackled. Mike's voice dipped in and out before the line disconnected.

"Mike! Mike? Are you there?" He looked at the screen. His signal dropped then reconnected to the network. He redialled again.

Mike's voice boomed through the speakers as the call connected. "I've got her. I've got Abby."

Scott choked. The breath caught in his throat as an emotional tidal wave surged through him. He wiped away the tears that blurred his vision. He slowed his car and pulled on to the verge. Scott cleared his throat, let out a deep sigh, and rested his head on the wheel.

"Is she okay?" he asked.

"Yes, guv. She looks rough around the edges... but then she does most days." Mike laughed, injecting his own inimitable style of humour. "We're in an ambulance and inbound to the Royal Sussex. I'll call you back in a second."

Scott frowned at the way the call ended, but then was taken by surprise when Mike's video call came through on WhatsApp. Scott hit the connect button and saw Abby's face. She sported heavy bruising to her forehead; dirty tear tracks stained her cheeks; lank, greasy hair was matted to the sides of her face.

"Now you know what Abby looks like first thing in the morning before she's put on a bit of slap," Mike said.

Scott smiled and blew out his cheeks in relief. "I'll

rendezvous with you later. I'm tracking North down. He did a runner from the barn before Helen and the troops arrived."

"Will do, guv. Are Cara and the baby okay?" Mike asked.

"I think so. The medics were checking her over and she will arrive at the Sussex not long after you. Once we've got North, I'll head over."

"Guv, don't go alone. He's already shown what he's capable of. He wants you, and God knows what he'll do if you come face to face with him."

"He's already been face to face with me, and he did shit. A rant and then he legged it. If he wanted a pop at me, he could have done it there and then in the barn. But he chose not to. Since the beginning he hasn't wanted to hurt me physically; he wanted to break me mentally and emotionally."

Scott hung up and sped off again, those last few words echoing in his mind. He was dealing with a man who had given up on life because his family meant everything to him. Without them, and in North's eyes, there was nothing else to live for. Rather than seek help to come to terms with that, he'd chosen to inflict the same mental and emotional torture that he was experiencing onto someone else.

59

Scott listened to a running commentary from officers back at the office as North's car pinged ANPR cameras travelling through Brighton. He had instructed officers to position themselves in unmarked cars at the entry and exit points to the cemetery and Bear Road to intercept North, whilst others were to make their way on foot to meet up with him.

The crematorium had just finished a service when Scott pulled into the cemetery and drove past the building. Relatives filed out in small huddles, arms looped, clutching tissues and dabbing their eyes. With members of the public close by, Scott couldn't afford to put their lives at risk or create a scene at such a sensitive moment for them.

He slowed and wove his way past the lines of gravestones that filled his vision as far as he could see, before coming to a stop close to Angel's Corner. Under the dappled canopy of a tree, he paused for a moment and scanned his surroundings for any movement. Officers hadn't reported North's vehicle arriving.

Safe knowing that North wasn't around, Scott exited his car and ran towards the sheltered resting place. Ornate gravestones filled his view, some small, others taller than him, many adorned with helium balloons, teddy bears, pictures, and fluffy toys. Parents had made permanent shrines for their little ones, a special place for families to gather and share memories of happier times.

It was a precious place for Scott. He had spent many moments talking to Becky, recalling happier times and mischievous moments that only she could have got away with.

To his right he saw a shadow moving at pace between the trees. One minute it was there, the next it was gone. Scott moved towards it. It was North. He was sure of it. The figure reappeared again from behind a large headstone and charged towards Becky's grave.

"Give it up!" Scott shouted, as he raced off in pursuit, dodging between the stones. "It's over!"

His shouts alerted officers who approached on foot, their pace quickening as they joined in the chase.

"It's never over. It never will be," North shouted over his shoulder, his hammer held high above his head as he closed in on Becky's grave.

Scott pushed on. Lactic acid made his legs feel like concrete blocks, but he pushed through, racing on a collision course with North which would end feet from Becky's remains. Scott could hear North panting as he closed the gap. With feet to go, Scott surged to come within touching distance of North. He lunged and grabbed North by the shoulders, bringing the man down.

The forward momentum caused Scott to roll over on to his back. It gave North the opportunity to scramble to his feet, pick up his hammer, and lunge at Becky's headstone a few feet away. Scott got back on his feet and raced after North again, tackling the man for a second time.

"Enough!" Scott growled, as he wrapped his arms around North's waist and head-butted the man's chest.

They both fell backwards onto a patch of grass between the adjoining stones. North raised his hammer and swung it at Scott's head; Scott raised his arm to deflect the blow. Not finished by a long shot, North jammed his knee into Scott's stomach to push him away. The shock of the impact caused Scott to wince, and pain bounced through his stomach and up into his ribs.

North rolled away but Scott grabbed the man's ankle with one hand, before locking his other hand around it too. North tried to rise to his feet, but fell when Scott tugged him back.

Scott spun around and grabbed North in a headlock, pushing him face down onto the ground. Every bone in his body wanted to squeeze the life out of this man. He felt his arm tightening around North's neck, an uncontrollable force taking over, telling him to finish the job. He ground his teeth as his muscles tensed, heat flashing through his body. His subconscious mind egged him on.

A voice deep within screamed and fantasised about a violent end. *Finish the job! Make this the last minute on earth for him!*

A smaller part of Scott wanted to show mercy as North thrashed on the ground, clawing at Scott's arm. North gurgled and squealed as he gasped for air. His heels dug in to the ground, desperate for traction to push Scott away. Scott continued to squeeze harder, the anger from the last few days, the torment and helplessness now pouring from him.

Scott's face twisted as he held on tight. His eyes flitted from one stone to another before pausing on Becky's grave, and a smiling picture of her. Electrical circuits connected in his brain; voices screamed at him; Becky's laughter echoed in his ears.

Backup arrived and officers piled in to pull North away.

Scott loosened his grip and fell back on his arse, gasping for breath as he stared at Becky's photo. Tears fell from his eyes.

Both men gasped for breath, one out of desperation to survive, the other from the desire to kill.

Scott blinked hard to push the tears from his eyes. He got to his feet and knelt beside North as the man's hands were handcuffed behind his back.

60

C ara's lids flickered open before closing again for a few moments. Her brain struggled to engage and process where she was. White ceiling. Glaring bright lights. Voices in the corridor. The sound of bleeping machines and trolleys rattling. The smell. A familiar smell of disinfectant.

She opened her eyes again and looked around the room. Everything hurt. Her legs, her back, her face. Glancing down at the bed, she noticed the dressings around her wrists. It was as if someone had pulled the plug on her life and all the energy had drained from her. Fogginess clouded her thoughts as she recalled the events of the last few days. *The tank. Water. Nearly drowning. People shouting. Being pulled out of the tank. The sirens. The ambulance.*

"Hey, morning," Scott said, as he leaned forward in his chair and held her hand. He stroked the back of her fingers with his thumb. Though the tips of his fingers were sore and covered in dressings, he hoped his touch reassured her.

Cara craned her neck to look up at Scott. She narrowed her eyes. *Scratches on his face and the bruising.*

"What happened to you?" she asked, licking her lips. Her voice was croaky, her lips dry and cracked.

"Shssh... don't you worry about me. I'm fine. You need to rest."

"Have you been here all night?" Cara asked. She furrowed her brow in concern.

Scott nodded and smiled, as he tipped his head to one side.

"You should have gone home. Jesus, what happened to you?" Cara said, as she lifted his hand to examine his dressings.

"As I said, don't worry about me. The main thing is that you're safe."

"The baby?" Cara asked. Worry lines creased her forehead as she searched Scott's face for an answer.

"The baby is fine. You've *both* been through an awful experience. You and the baby must be tough as old boots because the doctor said you'll both be fine. Other than dehydration, a touch of hypothermia and a few minor injuries, there's nothing for us to worry about."

Cara squeezed Scott's wrist. Her eyes moistened as her chin trembled. "Are they sure the baby is all right? Have they run all the tests? Have they done scans? Has the baby been stressed in any way?"

The questions came in rapid-fire, taking Scott by surprise. "The doctors will do their rounds in the next hour or two. We can get all our questions answered then. The doctor who dealt with you when you came in told the nurses that you and the baby were stable, and that you just needed plenty of rest whilst they monitored you for the next twenty-four to forty-eight hours."

Cara sighed and winced. Her whole body ached. She wasn't sure she'd be able to get out of the bed to go to the loo. She groaned when she saw the surgical pee bottle on the table beside her.

"Is Abby okay?"

"As far as I can tell, yes. I'm going to pop along and see her in a minute, if that's okay?"

"Of course. Send her my love when you see her. Maybe they can push us along in wheelchairs and we can meet in the middle of a corridor..." Cara smiled. She wanted to laugh but couldn't muster the energy.

They sat in a comfortable silence for a few minutes, neither wanting to steer the conversation to the elephant in the room until Cara pushed the matter.

"What's happened to *him*?"

"We arrested North. After he left the barn, he headed to the cemetery. His last act was an attempt to desecrate Becky's grave." Scott massaged his eyes and yawned, the tiredness creeping up on him. "He didn't set out to kill me. His intention was to inflict as much emotional and psychological pain on me as possible. Apparently, North wanted me to feel what he'd been feeling for over twenty years after he lost his family."

Cara remained quiet as Scott updated her. She thought there would be a dozen questions floating around in her mind, but there was nothing there. An emptiness remained. She felt numb. *It's shock. It has to be.* The thought crossed her mind whether she would still experience this strange disconnection in the days and weeks to come. Or would it hit her with the force of an express train that left her clinging to the bedcovers and not wishing to face the world?

"The main thing is he can't hurt us any more. He was a lone wolf and there was no one else involved as far as we can tell. You and I both have to focus on the future now. We need time to heal, mentally and physically." Scott stood and leaned in closer, kissing her on the lips. "My number one priority will be the safety of you and our baby. I promise. You get some rest whilst I see Abby."

Cara smiled weakly and closed her eyes.

61

Scott took a short walk along the corridor to Abby's room. He lingered outside, his fingers resting on the door. He didn't know what to say when he saw her. A ball of nerves sat in his stomach as he leaned into the door and stepped inside.

Abby clocked him the second he appeared. Her head was resting on a stack of pillows, the white sheet and blanket pulled up to her neck.

Scott hesitated in the doorway before making his way over to her bed. "How's the patient?"

"Like I have been on the most terrifying rollercoaster ride. Either that or I've fallen out of the ugly tree and hit every branch on the way down."

Scott dropped into the chair beside her bed. "You don't look that bad. Your bruises will fade. The cuts will heal. Before long you'll be back to your same annoying self." He tried to lighten the mood. He wasn't sure if it helped or made things worse, because tears filled Abby's eyes. "Hey, listen. You're going to be okay."

Spittle flew from her lips as the tears flowed. "My kids. I could have died. This bloody job." She clenched her teeth as her hands curled into fists.

Scott closed his eyes for a minute and looked at the floor. After everything Abby had said over recent months about walking away from the job, this had to happen. He had tried his hardest to hang on to Abby, including changing her shift patterns and delegating her work to Helen, to allow her to be at home more often with the kids. These small steps had appeased Abby and things were going so well... until North. The bastard had done this to Cara and Abby.

"I don't know what to say." He reached out and took her hand. "This is all my fault. I'm sorry. I wish I could turn back the clock and make this all go away. My actions led to the two people I care most about being abducted, held against their will, assaulted, and ending up in the hospital." He'd held it together whilst sitting with Cara, but seeing Abby only made him feel worse. He cleared his throat and wiped his eyes with the back of his hand.

"How did you find me?" she asked.

"After North abducted you, we found your personal mobile phone at the scene. Mike searched your desk and your home looking for your job phone. When he couldn't find it, he ran a search on the number and did a triangulation. It was then that we realised you had your job phone on you, and if North hadn't discovered it, we could use the coordinates to find you."

Abby squeezed his hand and sniffed loudly; snot dribbled from her nose. "I must look like the back end of a cow!" she said, sniffing again and blinking hard through red, puffy eyelids.

"Well, come to think of it…"

"Don't even go there. I see you got your fingers bandaged up. If they are not broken, they will be if you keep talking."

62

Scott felt a warm glow. He hadn't lost Abby completely. "We couldn't let North know we were tracking your phone signal. He knew it was impossible for me to be in two places at the same time. Even though he said he wanted to hurt me, it was clear from his intentions that if we continued to play by his rules, one of you would have died." He paused for a moment and stretched his back, to ease the ache. "We knew he would probably watch both locations. We weren't certain what kind of improvised devices he had rigged up, so I asked Mike to go dark and track you down."

Abby nodded and rolled her eyes.

Scott continued. "His days in the military proved invaluable. He made his way covertly to your location, scoped the scene, did his reconnaissance and only went in when he was confident. Time wasn't on our side, so he couldn't wait for reinforcements. He spotted the camera trap by the entrance and stayed out of its field of view."

Abby held Scott's hand. Just the connection helped to calm her fear and anxiety.

"Your kids are downstairs in the canteen. They're being well looked after. They're desperate to see you, so shall I ring down and tell them to come up?"

Abby nodded. "What about North?"

"Meadows did the interview. They gathered a tonne of evidence against him. A search of his property revealed fibres from the clothing he wore when abducting Cara. It had Cara's DNA on it. They recovered a van belonging to him. Again, Cara's DNA was identified in the cargo bay and on a blanket."

"Perfect," Abby muttered.

Scott nodded in agreement. "The search team also discovered envelopes matching those we received and a petrol receipt from Hastings. A right Aladdin's cave of treasure." He guffawed. "North confessed to all of it. He said he had nothing to hide. We're charging him with two counts of abduction and imprisonment, and one count of assaulting an emergency worker. That's just for starters. Add to that, vandalism and desecration of..." Scott's voice trailed off as sadness filled him.

"I'm sorry, Scott. You didn't deserve any of this either. Your family deserved to rest in peace," Abby said.

"Yeah, I know. Cara and I need to talk. I don't know what the future holds for us. I need to make sure that she stays safe and well, for her sake and the baby's. The force will offer Cara their counselling services. They'll offer you the same before you can return."

Abby remained quiet whilst she processed her own thoughts. "I need to sit down with my kids as well. I've made my feelings clear about the job. What happened to me is a step too far in my book. My kids could have lost their mother. I need to think about whether I can continue being a frontline officer."

Scott chewed on his bottom lip as she hit him with the news he dreaded. He was as confused as Abby. Was the job worth putting their own lives and those of their family at risk?

"You could always do civilian support?" he suggested. "Or retire early and come back as a civilian officer working on CID cases?"

Abby shrugged, as she stared at the blank wall in front of her. The answers eluded her right now.

"Besides, there's no point thinking about it," Scott added. "All you need at the moment is rest and recovery. You need time to come to terms with what you've been through. Don't rush it. Let the answers come naturally." He stood up.

Abby continued to hold his hand, not wanting to let go. She looked at Scott as more tears filled her eyes. "Thank you."

"For what? Putting you in hospital?" He grinned.

Abby chewed her lip. There was so much she wanted to say but knew it would likely tumble from her mouth in one long, incoherent dribble. "Well not for this, no. But for being the best friend I could ever ask for. You mean a lot to me and I'm glad you're safe." She squeezed his hand.

Scott shrugged and held her gaze.

"Cara's very lucky to have you as her partner, and I'm lucky to have you as my friend. Will you pop in and see me later?"

"Try keeping me away," Scott replied.

63

One week later.

It felt like the first day at a new school as Scott made his way through the station. News of the ordeal that Scott, Cara, and Abby had been through was on everyone's lips. The canteen discussions and the idle chat on patrol all focused on the events that had rocked Brighton nick and Sussex Police. For many officers, this was the first time they had seen Scott since North's capture and the safe return of Cara and Abby.

Questions and comments hit him from every angle. It was hard to keep track of who was saying what, which only overwhelmed him. "Good to see you back." "You're looking well, guv." "How are you holding up?"

He felt humbled that so many officers he rarely met on a day-to-day basis had walked up to him and shook his hand, passing on their best wishes.

Scott paused at the door to CID and took a deep breath, as his mind flipped back over the last few days. Life at home had been challenging following Cara's return. She slipped from periods of quiet reflection to episodes of uncontrollable tears, to moments where she seemed like her old self. An officer from the Welfare Unit had visited Scott and Cara. Their conversation confirmed in Scott's mind that his return to work would be a long and arduous process.

Composing himself, he pushed open the door. He was instantly greeted by a round of applause from a crowded room of officers, many squeezing into tight spots to get a better vantage point.

The reaction took Scott by surprise. Mike, Helen and Raj stepped forward to greet him. Mike, in his own inimitable way, gave Scott a healthy slap on the arm, before embracing him in a powerful hug more befitting of a Greco-Roman wrestler attacking his opponent.

"Good to see you again, guv. The desk sergeant told us you were on your way up," Mike said, as he stepped back.

Raj did the same, but his hug wasn't as intense, which gave Scott the chance to get breath back into his lungs.

Helen followed and gave him the softest embrace before shuffling back, overcome with emotion.

Scott smiled at her. "I can't tell you what an integral part you played in helping to rescue Cara and Abby. You went above and beyond. I admire you for that and owe you an enormous debt of gratitude."

A few officers cheered and another round of applause erupted around the room.

Helen's cheeks flushed as she batted away the compliment. "I'm glad I could help. Thank you for trusting me."

Scott gathered the team. Everyone huddled in close, their attention fixed on him.

"I want to thank each one of you for your tireless work, commitment, and dedication. Your efforts saved two people, and I'll never be able to find the right words to express how proud I am of you all." Scott scanned the sea of faces. Many smiled, a few dabbed their eyes, and guys like Mike puffed out their chests, determined not to show their softer side.

"I'm going to be away a little while longer whilst Cara and I process what's happened. I think we're due a little time off. In the meantime, keep up the amazing work."

Scott backed away as more applause erupted. He waved them away. "Go. Get on with your work. I'm going to see the boss."

64

Scott hesitated in the hallway outside Meadows's office, strategising about what to say. He'd thought about it and rehearsed it in his mind a dozen times on his journey to the station, but so much confusion clouded his judgement that nothing seemed to make sense.

"Sir..." Scott said, as he stood in the open doorway.

Meadows looked up and swiftly rose from his chair before coming around his desk to greet Scott at the door. He shook Scott's hand like a long-lost friend, which Scott found odd.

"Good to see you, Scott. I'm glad you've come in. Take a seat."

"Thank you, sir."

Meadows grabbed the chair opposite and smiled. He took a few moments to study Scott. "How are you holding up?"

Although Meadows meant well, Scott must have heard the same question a hundred times that morning. "I'm doing okay, sir. I'm still trying to get my head around everything."

Meadows nodded and pursed his lips, feeling sympathy for his inspector. "And Cara?"

Scott shrugged. "Your guess is as good as mine. She has good and bad moments. I'm worried about what effect it's having on her and the baby. Stress and emotional anxiety can affect both of them."

"Have you spoken to anyone?"

"Yes, I've raised it with the midwife and doctor to see what support *we* can give her. I've so much to do. I'm not looking forward to it but we're moving Tina's remains to a different plot. That's going to hit hard. I can't go back to the same spot; it doesn't feel right. But this new location is nearer to Becky too."

"Well, if there's anything I can do to help, you only have to ask." Meadows paused for a moment and sighed. "Listen, Scott, I know we haven't always seen eye to eye, and I can sound like a cantankerous fool sometimes, and you can be a bit... cavalier, but I'm truly sorry for what has happened to you, Cara... and Abby. We do the job to make a difference. To protect lives and uphold the law. What happened to you was unjustified, vile, and abhorrent."

"Thank you, sir. It means a lot."

Meadows dropped his shoulders. "I visited Abby yesterday. I'm concerned about her. She doesn't have a strong support network so I'm relying on our welfare team, myself, and the rest of your team to get her through this. She's taken extended leave whilst considering her options. And that's understandable." He raised his hands in acknowledgement. "I was thinking of making Mike acting DS in her absence. What do you think?"

"I think that's a good call, sir. With Raj and Helen supporting him, it's a good temporary fix."

"Good. Good. I'll get that organised. And what about yourself? What are your plans for returning? I don't mean to rush you. That's not why I'm asking. I want you to take all the time you need."

Scott stared at his shoes, trying to find the right words. He looked up. "Sir, I'm not sure I'm coming back."

Meadows's eyes widened. He sat back in his chair, surprise written all over his face. "Um... um... okay. You've been through a harrowing experience. I appreciate you're still trying to make sense of what's happened. Can I suggest you don't make any rash decisions until it's clear in your own mind what you want? Does that make sense?"

"It does, sir. I lost one family and buried them. I nearly lost another. My priority has to be the welfare of my partner and our baby. For the first time in many years, I feel like my old self. I have Cara to thank for that. She's a wonderful woman and without her, my life would be one lonely place."

"Well... I guess I can... draft in a DI from another team to cover for you."

"Thank you. Sir, I've decided to take indefinite leave. I hope you can respect that. We need time to heal." Scott rose and extended his hand to Meadows.

Meadows shook Scott's hand firmly. "I hope you reach the right decision for you and your family. I'm here if you need to talk. In the meantime, don't be a stranger. I'm sure the team will miss you as much as the rest of the station. Keep in touch."

Scott turned and left. As he walked along the corridor and down the steps towards the car park, a sense of relief washed over him. With that decision made, a heavy weight had been lifted off his shoulders. He pushed through the back door and exited into the car park where he blew out his cheeks and stared up at the sky.

Scott pulled the phone from his pocket and dialled Cara's number.

"Scottie? Is everything okay?"

"It's fine. It's more than fine. I'm coming home."

WE HOPE YOU ENJOYED THIS BOOK

If you could spend a moment to write an honest review on Amazon, no matter how short, we would be extremely grateful. They really do help readers discover new authors.

ALSO BY JAY NADAL

TIME TO DIE

(Book 1 in the DI Scott Baker series)

THE STOLEN GIRLS

(Book 2 in the DI Scott Baker series)

ONE DEADLY LESSON

(Book 3 in the DI Scott Baker series)

IN PLAIN SIGHT

(Book 4 in the DI Scott Baker series)

AN EVIL OFFERING

(Book 5 in the DI Scott Baker series)

EYE FOR AN EYE

(Book 6 in the DI Scott Baker series)

MARKED FOR DEATH

(Book 7 in the DI Scott Baker series)

DIE FOR ME

(Book 8 in the DI Scott Baker series)

LEAVE NO TRACE

(Book 9 in the DI Scott Baker series)

THE FINAL REVENGE

(Book 10 in the DI Scott Baker series)

'

Printed in Great Britain
by Amazon